Splatology

Unveiling Nightmares Ltd

UNVEILING NIGHTMARES
CRAFTING NIGHTMARES, ONE TALE AT A TIME

Copyright © 2024 by Unveiling Nightmares
All rights belong to the authors for their contributed works.
No portion of this book may be reproduced in any form without written
permission from the publisher or author,
except as permitted by U.K copyright law.
Editor Sidney Shiv
Cover Grim Poppy Designs

Trigger Warnings

Well... What can I say...
There are a lot.
If you can't hack it, *don't fucking read it.*

Contents

1. Amphetamines And Smegma — 1
2. Mommy's Bowels — 21
3. Scalped Soup — 53
4. The Professional — 69
5. And He was Forsaken — 99
6. Feed the Earth — 111
7. Full Nasty — 121
8. Turduckin' — 153
9. You Have a New Message — 187
10. Midnight at the Dead Dick, Fuck-hole Emporium — 217
11. Blood Harvest — 253

Acknowledgements — 276

Amphetamines And Smegma

By Jason Nickey

As Rock drove down the interstate, only one thing was on his mind: the cargo in his trailer. As he thought to himself, he wondered if he'd been overzealous this past week. As an independent owner-operator truck driver, he could take contracts as he pleased, often taking time off to have fun. Unlike most truck drivers, though, he still spent his off time on the road.

It was what he enjoyed. It was when he could 'play'.

The fact that he didn't have a house to pay a mortgage or rent on, along with not having a wife or kids, gave him this freedom. The cab of his truck was his home on wheels, allowing him to never stay in one place for too long.

He enjoyed seeing parts of the country most others would never get to see, and he found both good and bad with every state he had been to, which happened to be all of them except Hawaii and Alaska. If you asked him to pick his favorite, his answer would be Oklahoma.

He had a pre-programmed variety of answers he would use when anyone asked why that was his favorite, but only he knew the real reason. Oklahoma was where he discovered his new passion, his new hobby.

It all started about five years ago...

As a truck driver, he understandably spent a lot of time at truck stops and rest areas. These areas were known to be places where you would find lot lizards: women who enjoyed making lonely truck driver types feel good for a night—or maybe just a few minutes, depending on the arrangement. These arrangements usually involved a money exchange as well. Rock was okay with that, but he preferred the ones who didn't charge him as much to dump a load in one of their holes.

It went without saying the women who did this weren't exactly classy. This was in no way a deterrent for Rock. He typically preferred his women on the trashy side. They were often more open to suggestions—more willing to let him do what he wanted without complaint.

Rock wasn't exactly what most would consider conventionally attractive. He was a large-framed man, built like a football player but with a lot more belly. A victim of male pattern baldness, he was completely bald on top, typically sporting a ratty ring of hair along the sides and back of his head. His shaggy beard was completely unkempt, not grown for style but out of laziness and the need to cover some of the pockmark scars on his face.

His head and face weren't the only parts of him sporting unkempt hair, as his body was about as hairy as a gorilla. He would occasionally run into women who were turned on by this. But most were not fans, especially since the mass of body hair often held onto the odor he acquired going multiple days without a shower.

All things considered, he couldn't be picky about his women, especially if he chose ones who didn't charge too much. He had grown to be turned on by seeing the disgust in women's faces while he was thrusting his member inside them.

The night in question was a rainy summer night in an Oklahoma truck stop. He had just been unloaded at a local warehouse and had pulled in for a night's rest. He planned to begin a week off before his next contracted load. To celebrate, he had decided to start his little vacation by getting his dick wet.

He knew the game, and he knew how to play it. Sitting in his driver's seat with the window down, he lit a cigarette and smoked it slowly, sure to hold the butt out of the window to allow the bright red cherry to act as a beacon of sorts, a sign that someone was awake and looking. This was an unspoken code in these places, and it usually didn't take long for someone to stroll by.

It wasn't long before a woman walked past. A skinny little thing in a short skirt, tank top, high heels, and enough makeup to make a drag queen look like an amateur. She stopped as she passed and stepped back to confirm that she had seen the lit cigarette hanging out of the window.

As she approached, he could tell by her disheveled appearance that she had just been ridden hard by another trucker. This never bothered him much, as he never minded sloppy seconds. As long as he was getting his, that was all that mattered.

"You lookin,' big guy?" She asked as she stood by his window.

"I might be," he replied.

"My stash is running low, and I could use some extra dough tonight to get more."

"What can I get for fifty?" he asked with the grin of a fiend.

"Honey, I'm running a special tonight. Make it seventy-five, and you can do whatever you want."

Rock couldn't tell if she was naïve and unaware of how nasty some truckers could get or if she was the type who didn't mind degrading herself, if need be, to get the money she needed. Regardless, he took her up on her offer and leaned over to pull the handle on the passenger door. He watched her as she walked over, thinking of how nasty he wanted to get with her.

He could tell by her struggle for balance as she climbed into the truck that she was already high. She tipped forward slightly as she entered the cab, revealing she wasn't wearing a bra under her tank top. She was seemingly fearless as he motioned his hand for her to step into the back. He got out of his seat and stepped in behind her, pulling the privacy curtain closed behind him.

Since it was already dark outside, it didn't take them long to adjust to the dim, dull glow of the dome light that lit the cab. Rock stripped off his clothes and sat on the bed while the woman stood there.

"Take off your clothes," He commanded sternly but not too aggressively.

She complied. He could tell by the smoothness of her motions that she was an old pro. He could often tell the girls who were newer to the game, as they were typically shaky and nervous, at least at the beginning of the encounter.

"Turn around and bend over."

She did as she was told. Before she could ask him what he wanted her to do next, he barked out, "Now spread those cheeks. Show me those holes."

One look at her pussy confirmed his earlier suspicion that she had just been worked over by someone else at the truck stop. It looked as if she was still dripping a bit of cum from her previous suitor.

Rock leaned back on his elbows, his dick almost throbbing as it pointed straight up. "Get on your hands and knees and crawl towards me, slowly, until my cock is in your mouth."

She crawled towards him, making her best attempt at a seductive motion, which wasn't very good. He chuckled to himself as she approached his cock and took pause, knowing what her hesitation was. With his foreskin receding down his growing erection, she could see the smegma slathered around the head of his dick. It had been three days since his last shower.

"Clean it off," he said, pulling his foreskin back.

Like a pro, she took a deep breath and went for it. He could feel her holding back occasional gags as she worked her mouth back and forth, working her tongue around the head of his cock and cleaning beneath his foreskin. The warmth of her mouth felt great, and Rock moaned in pleasure.

Getting off of his elbows, Rock lay back and put his right hand on the back of her head as she bobbed on his cock. He smiled at the thought of his next move, which he was just about ready for.

Feeling the pressure building up, he pushed down on the back of her head, forcing her all the way down to the base. This led her to believe he was about to come.

Holding her there, he released the pressure he had felt, letting out a large ripper of a fart. It resonated loudly, like a trumpet, and he felt her flinch as it happened. He laughed, knowing she was doing her best to ignore the rank smell that was no doubt invading her nostrils. He could smell it himself. It was quite a nasty brew.

Once the smell in the cab had dissipated some, he pulled her head back by the hair, his cock making a popping noise as it came out of her mouth.

He sat straight up and slowly stood. "On the bed. On your back."

She did as he instructed, and he climbed on the bed, lifting her legs and positioning himself in front of her.

Positioning her legs as close to her face as he could get them, he instructed her to hold them there. He then shoved his cock inside her and leaned forward, letting his upper body weight rest on his hands beside her as he pounded away. He began sweating profusely, raining on her as he thrust into her with all he had. His breathing intensified as he got close, and knowing his breath had to be horrible at this point, he made sure every exhalation was aimed directly at her face.

He was just about to come when he leaned in closer as if to kiss her. Only kissing her wasn't what he had in mind. As she began to position her mouth to meet his kiss, he let out a loud belch in her face. Her disgusted reaction to this caused him to blow his load inside her.

Panting as he finished, he collapsed on top of her, knowing his weight was too much for her small frame to handle. He lay there for just a few moments, feeling her struggling to breathe before lifting his body off of hers and sitting up to light a cigarette.

He lit a second one and offered it to her. She didn't say a word as she took it, but he could tell she was pissed off at his rudeness. This was always his favorite part of an encounter, knowing they had to continue to be nice because they wanted payment.

Looking down at the floor, he noticed a baggie sticking out of the pocket of the woman's shorts. He reached down and snagged it, revealing what looked to be a decent amount of crystal.

"I thought you said your stash was low," he said with a laugh. "A liar and a whore."

She quickly snatched the bag from his hand in a defensive manner. "If you must know," she stated, a bit of attitude in her tone. "This was a front—a front I have to pay back by tomorrow. I don't exactly like to advertise that I have this much on me. Some folks like to take what isn't theirs."

"Fair enough," Rock said with a nod. "How much more do you need to pay it off?"

"With what you owe me, I'll need another hundred."

Rock nodded. "What if you could have that extra hundred in the next half hour and be done for the night?"

"What did you have in mind?" she asked suspiciously.

An evil grin spread across Rock's face before he leaned in and told her. She cringed as he spoke, but reluctantly, she nodded, accepting his offer. "Just let me finish this smoke first... and pay me up-front."

Rock nodded.

A few minutes later, she snubbed the cigarette in his ashtray and pulled a small glasses case from her pocket. She opened the case and removed a spoon and a syringe. Rock laughed to himself as she loaded the spoon and held a lighter below it. He watched as the grainy substance began to melt and liquify before bubbling up and being sucked up into the syringe.

He was surprised that she didn't even flinch as the needle pierced her skin. A look of relief took over her face as she pushed the plunger and injected the amphetamine into her veins.

Wasting no time, Rock lay her on her back and positioned himself over top of her, slowly sitting on her face. He could feel her cringe as the bits of toilet paper clinging to his ass hair touched her tongue, dissolving upon contact with her saliva. He could feel her holding back gags as her tongue made its way around his poorly wiped anus. She was clearly making every effort to get past the bitter, earthy taste of his fecal residue as she worked her tongue around his hemorrhoids in the same manner a man would with a woman's clitoris.

He was starting to get hard again and enjoy himself as he degraded her when he noticed her body start to twitch. She began making a funny sound, and he pulled away, looking back to see what was wrong. By the time he got off of the bed and closer to her face, she was already gone, having overdosed on the shot of crank.

He got curious as he sat there, wondering how to handle the situation. Grabbing her baggie, he dumped a little bit on his hand, just between his thumb and forefinger, and snorted it. A bitter taste accompanied the burning sensation in his sinuses as the back drip trickled down his throat. He cringed at the taste but smiled as he felt the drug begin working its magic.

Before long, he felt exhilarated and full of energy. His heart began racing, and he felt more alive than he had in his fifty years. His cock grew rock hard again, and he looked over at the dead woman once more.

Climbing up onto the bed with her, he threw her legs over his shoulders and put his cock into her once again. He began thrusting, occasionally stopping to smack at her face, amused at the lack of reaction. He didn't know what had come over him, but he was more turned on than he'd ever been. He couldn't tell if it was the drug, the dead woman, or the combination of the two, but he had never felt more alive.

He left the next day, keeping the woman in his truck as he drove from state to state, occasionally stopping to fuck her again. This continued for a few days until the smell started getting to him. The week was almost over by the time he pulled over on the shoulder of a barren Indiana highway and dragged her body into the woods, leaving it there to rot under the trees.

Rock found himself sitting at another truck stop about a month later, beginning another week off from pick-ups and deliveries. He still had the baggie of crank the woman had left behind. He hadn't touched it since that night, as he was saving it for his next encounter.

He pulled it out and did a quick bump before lighting a cigarette and hanging it out the window, signaling that he was looking.

As was usually the case, it wasn't long before his hook got a snag, and he reeled one in. Twenty minutes later, he made a proposition, which was accepted, and he was shoving his dick into another trashy woman in the cab of his truck.

Something was different this time, though. The whole encounter seemed lackluster, and he was having trouble maintaining his erection.

Getting frustrated, an idea popped into his head. He grabbed the pillow from beneath the woman's head and held it over her face. He lay on her, putting all of his weight on her body to keep her from escaping. She clawed and grabbed at him, trying to escape. He yelped as she pulled on some of his back hair but kept the pressure on the pillow.

Eventually, she stopped moving. His cock throbbed at the realization that the woman was dead. And like the woman before, he began fucking her after she passed. Just as he had before, he continued fucking her corpse over the next few days until the smell got to him, and he had to dispose of her, this time in a cornfield running along the interstate in Kansas.

Over time, he fine-tuned his craft and came up with more creative ways to kill and dispose of the women—sometimes striking them with blunt objects, sometimes offering them drugs laced with fatal additives. When he wanted to get messy, he would take them into the trailer and use a knife on them, later finding a safe place to hose out the blood.

This past week, though, he had become overzealous in his desire to improve his game. He had set a plan in motion that he'd been working on for a while. Having been gun-shy about acting on this plan, he finally bit the bullet on Thursday night and began step one.

Parked at a truck stop in Texas, he picked up a woman in his usual manner. His plan from the get-go was to kill her, but he had focused so much on the killing part lately that he was starting to miss some of the degrading things he used to do, so he decided to have a little fun first.

Shortly after he began killing women, he acquired what was basically an adult-sized potty to keep in the cab of his truck. This made it so that when he was driving around with a dead woman, he could make fewer pit stops in public places and reduce the risk of being caught. As this woman, aptly named Trish, approached his truck, he remembered that the potty in the cab of the truck had not been emptied from the massive bowel movement he'd had earlier that morning. One look at Trish, a bit older than his usual fare, told him she was far from new to the game and had probably seen it all. She would be perfect for what he wanted to do.

It wasn't long before he had her on all fours, pounding her from behind while holding her head in the hole of the potty seat, making her take in the sight and smell of his stale morning piss and a massive pile of shit. She gagged as he fucked her and eventually threw up, adding to the disgusting stew within his adult potty.

While it wasn't quite as exciting for him as fucking a dead woman, feeling her muscles contract and put a kung-fu grip on his cock as she vomited made him come almost as hard.

Once he was finished, she turned to him. Beads of sweat glistened on her forehead, a bit of drool hung from her lip, and she was breathing heavily from vomiting. He offered her a bump of his 'special stuff' for her troubles. She accepted his offer, and once she caught her breath, did a line of his tainted crank.

She was dead within minutes, and in his excitement, he fucked her again. He was tempted to have a third go at her before calling it a night but decided to save some energy for the next day.

Waiting until the dead of night, he went outside to make sure the coast was clear before opening the rear of the trailer, carrying her body to it, and laying it on the floor of the nose.

The next day, he drove to a truck stop in Oklahoma, which, in his mind, was the perfect place to take the next step in his plan. At the same rest area where his new fetish began, he picked up another woman. This time, when she entered the truck, he grabbed her from behind and put a cloth over her face. The chemicals on the cloth made her dizzy for a moment before she eventually passed out.

After laying her on the floor, he returned to the driver's seat and put the truck in gear. He drove down the highway to an empty pull-off he had discovered a while back. It was on a desolate road in the middle of nowhere and would be the perfect place for the privacy of what he wanted to do.

As the woman came to, she woke to discover that her hands and feet had been tied together. She began to flail, trying to break free as he carried her to the rear of the trailer, where the doors sat open.

After laying her down again, he climbed in, lit a lantern, and closed the door behind him. He carried the lantern to the nose of the trailer beside Trish's body before heading back to the rear to grab this new woman.

It took the woman a moment to realize the body next to her was dead. She screamed as soon as it dawned on her. Rock aptly punched her hard in the face and held a knife to her throat.

"You'll do exactly as I say if you want to get out of this alive. You understand me?"

She didn't respond at first, so Rock pressed the blade a little harder against her throat.

"I said, do you understand me?"

Through tears, she nodded.

Rock positioned her on her elbows and knees, getting behind her as he prepared to fuck her doggy style. She gasped and began to whimper as he slid his cock inside her.

As he began to fuck her, he grabbed her by the ribs and slowly inched her forward, scooting himself forward with her until her head was between Trish's spread legs.

"Eat it!" He commanded.

She began sobbing.

He held the tip of the knife against her back. "Put your tongue in that dead cunt, or I'll end the night by cleaning your insides from the back of this truck."

Reluctantly, she complied. She cried and took staggered, gasping breaths as she unenthusiastically performed cunnilingus on the dead woman.

"Fuck yes!" Rock exclaimed as he thrust harder, bringing himself close to orgasm. The putrid smell and knowing the woman had her tongue in the corpse's rotten pussy turned him on.

Just as he was about to come, he reached down and pushed her face as hard as he could into the dead woman's cunt. She began to vomit, and he let out a howl as he shot his load inside her, reveling in her disgust.

Rock leaned back to catch his breath. He was in awe at the excitement this new encounter had brought him. It distracted him just long enough for the woman to stand up and make a run for it. With her legs tied up, she couldn't move very quickly.

Thinking fast, he dove for her and grabbed her ankle, bringing her to the floor before she made it halfway down the trailer. Climbing on top of her, he sat on the small of her back and pulled her up in a backward arch by her hair. Bringing his mouth to her ear, he laughed.

"Wrong move, bitch," he said before slamming her face to the floor as hard as he could.

Having planned it out so there would be as little mess as possible, he reached over to the wall and grabbed the roll of pallet shrink wrap he'd placed there earlier. Pulling out the free end, he began wrapping the plastic around her face, sealing it tight, cutting off her air supply.

She grabbed for it a few times in her struggle for survival but ultimately became too weak and eventually died from lack of oxygen. He held her there for a while, ensuring she was gone before dragging her back to the nose of the trailer and placing her beside Trish.

He spent the rest of the night like a kid in a candy store, alternating as he fucked both women numerous times. It was the most excitement he'd felt since that first night in Oklahoma. He dreaded the inevitable moment when he would have to dispose of them because of their stench.

He slept through most of the next day, waking much later than planned. In a hurry, he checked outside and was relieved that the pull-off he was sitting in was still empty. He started the truck, put it in gear, and then got back on the road. He headed east to lay low for a while.

As he drove on through the night, his mind kept wandering to the two dead women in the trailer. All he could focus on was finding a quiet place to pull off and have more fun with them.

In his distraction, he didn't notice the two boys on the overpass he was about to drive under. He barely registered its existence, so the brown delivery sailing down from above, only to splatter across his windshield, caught him off guard.

Unsure of what had happened or if he had hit something, he slammed on his brakes. As the trailer's tail swung out, he did his best to correct the situation, but to no avail. The trailer's momentum caused his entire truck to flip on its side, completely blocking the highway. He cursed angrily, ignoring his pain at the thought of this stupid accident getting him caught.

He pushed the button to unbuckle his seatbelt, but it wouldn't give way. In a panic, he began pushing it harder, with the same results. He reached for his glove box and opened it. The contents spilled onto the passenger-side door, which was against the ground.

The knife he had aimed to grab from the glove box lay on the door, just out of his reach. He pulled at the seatbelt for more slack, but the belt caught almost immediately with each pull.

He almost gave up, but suddenly, an idea struck. He reached down and pulled the bar to adjust the seat. It only moved back about an inch, just enough to allow him to lean down and grip the knife with his fingertips.

"Fuck yes!" He shouted as he retrieved the knife and began cutting the seatbelt.

Finally, he was free. He climbed out the open window beside him. A few cars were stopped behind his overturned truck. In the distance, he could see red and blue lights approaching.

He jumped from the trailer and grunted as he landed on the pavement with a thud. His ankle cracked upon landing, sending a lightning bolt of pain up his leg.

"Fuck!" he screamed as he attempted to stand, immediately falling back to the ground.

At that moment, he wished he still had the knife so he could end it all before the police saw what was in the back of his truck.

Mommy's Bowels
By Chisto Healy

Milo watched with wide eyes as his mother tried to reach the grate above them with the fecal-encrusted skeletal arm. The bony fingers found the holes in the metal but had no way to grasp them and just bent backward. The digits snapped and fell back into the filth they were wading in. Milo watched as his mother screamed and charged the rock wall of their living space. She continued to scream and attacked the solid dirt wall with the human arm. The radius and the ulna broke away and fell into the shit-smelling mud at their feet. She continued to scream and smash the wall with the humerus until the dirt started to fall away.

"You're doing it, Mommy," Milo said. "You're breaking it!"

The dirt and rock crumbled underneath the weight of her fury. It invigorated her and drove her to attack even harder. Her throat was raw from screaming. She was spitting blood, and all Milo could do was look on with hope.

They had been down in this pit for three days and needed to go home. He was so tired, so sore, and nauseous from the terrine odor. Mommy said it was a waterless well they had been put in. Milo only knew one person with a well; all he saw in their yard was a big fake rock. He had no idea what a real well was like, so he had no way to know if Mommy was right or not.

The wall came away with a crash. Dirt and dust fell like a tidal wave over Mommy and buried her. The worst part was the dirt was not alone. As it fell towards them, it came with corpses. Empty, colorless eyes and withered grey flesh poured out of the broken wall. Her mouth was open mid-scream when the avalanche happened. Dead fingers reached for her. A dead woman's jaw came away and smacked her in the forehead as a decrepit rotting penis found its way into her open mouth. She gagged and fell beneath the wave of mud.

"Mommy?" Milo asked.

When he didn't get an answer, he cautiously approached the mound of dirt. Worms and beetles crawled about like everything was normal. Milo started crying. He didn't know what to do. Then he saw fingers protruding from the dirt that weren't rotted. "Mommy!"

He started to dig, but the more he dug, the more the dirt from the mound slid forward to fill the space. Now Milo was screaming like his mother. He started tearing at the corpses, trying to pull them off of the pile.

He had never seen an actual dead person before—well, his grandma, but he didn't think she counted because she didn't look real when he saw her. She was so covered in makeup she looked like a doll, and she was so stiff and inhuman in her casket.

This was completely different. These people were falling apart, and they stunk. Some were fresher than others, and strange gases billowed from their bloated bodies, adding more horrible odors to the unbreathable air.

As Milo grabbed a corpse to remove it, his tiny hands went right into the damn thing, popping the skin like a pimple and releasing old back blood that resembled tar. He screamed and tried to pull away, but his hands were stuck inside the thing, pinned between useless rotted organs. "Mommy!" he cried.

Milo fell backward, dragging the dead man with him. He fell on his back, and the body came with him, falling onto him in all its nakedness. Its newly opened torso spilled organs that slipped and slid on the ground around him.

When the dead man came free from the pile, Milo heard a gasp. He couldn't see, but he hoped it was his mother.

The corpse was too heavy to push off, so all he could do was lay there and cry.

Then, the dead thing was lifted and cast to the side. Milo looked up. His mother stood there, doubled over and panting. One of her eyes was wrong. The white was all red now, and he thought some of her teeth were broken. Strings of bloody drool hung from her battered mouth.

"Mommy?"

"Goddamn dead bastard's dick went right in my mouth."

"I'm sorry," Milo said, sitting up.

"It's alright, baby. It probably saved my life. If that rotten dick hadn't been there, my mouth would have filled with dirt. Oh God..."

"What, Mommy?"

She grabbed the wall and vomited. The projectile torrent spewed from her like the possessed casting out evil. When the puke came, Milo rushed to help her, and it showered him, raining down over him. The only food they'd had in the three days they were stuck down here was slabs of rotten meat the monster had thrown down. Chunks of it smacked his face and head and slid down in the mustard-colored mush.

Milo made the same mistake as his mother and screamed upon impact. Her throw-up filled his mouth and nostrils, and he gagged. Mommy was on her knees. It was still coming out of her, but she turned away from him. It sickened him even more to hear it as it seemed to be torn from her violently with horrible retching noises.

Milo tried to wipe his face. The vomit had gotten in his eyes, and it stung something awful. He couldn't breathe, so he tried to get the puke out of his nose. He held one nostril and blew with the other, spraying chunks of old meat lodged within. Then he did the other. His stomach lurched when his nose was unclogged, and he smelled the combination of putrid stenches consuming their area.

He had only a moment of warning before he erupted, spewing the contents of his stomach onto the pile. He gripped his stomach and leaned over, streams of sandy-looking drool hanging from his quivering lips. Thick snot hung from the tip of his nose, swaying back and forth like a pendulum.

His mother reached for him, trying to brush off what she could, running her hands through the wetness of his hair. She pulled a bite of chewed meat from his ear. "Oh baby, my baby, I'm so sorry," she said.

"I want to go home," Milo said, falling into her. She sat against the dirt wall amid the pile of vomit, shit, and rotting human entrails, and she held her boy close.

"I know, baby. I do, too. I do, too."

"Why is he doing this to us? Why are we down here?"

"I don't know, sweetheart. Some people are just bad, I guess."

"Are we gonna die down here?"

"No, baby. No. I won't let that happen. I promise. Somehow, some way, I'm going to get you out of here."

"Promise?"

"I do. "

Three Days Ago

Milo watched Mommy and Daddy kiss. He looked away toward the car as if he could move them with his gaze. "Have a good day. Be careful," Daddy said from the doorway.

"We will," Mommy said back.

Daddy came over then and kneeled before Milo. He looked him in the eyes. "I want you to be strong today, okay, Champ? Don't let those other kids push you around."

"Okay," Milo said, and he hoped his father didn't know as definitively as he did that it wasn't true. Milo had no intention of standing up to anyone.

"Attaboy," Daddy said, mussing Milo's brown mop of scraggly hair. "I know it's scary, but sometimes you have to do things you don't want to do in order to grow and become the man you're meant to be. Understand?"

"Yes, Daddy," Milo said. He understood that his father did, in fact, know he was lying.

"See you when I get home from work," Daddy said.

Milo watched him go to his truck. He liked the way Mommy smiled at Daddy when he came and went. He hoped someone would look at him like that when he was big. Milo grabbed his backpack and waited for Mommy to lock up. Then he hurried to the car. She had told him they could stop for pretzels on the way to school if they left early enough. They weren't the crunchy pretzels you could buy in the store but the big soft ones that were hot and salty—the ones you had to get from a vendor on the road.

"It's okay. We still have time," Mommy said, shining her smile his way. She was so pretty. Her eyes were like stars. Milo climbed into the passenger seat, placing his backpack on the floor. When Mommy was beside him and they were driving, she asked, "You want to tell me what's going on at school? What was your Dad talking about?"

"The other kids pick on me. I don't want to talk about it."

"Okay. Maybe later."

They got pretzels from the man with the stand under the big yellow umbrella. Milo and Mommy walked along the trail since the pretzel man was at the park. "Let's sit here so we're not too far from the car. We don't want to be late for school," she said.

Milo followed her and sat on a big rock. It was cool and made him feel like a pirate. He pretended the grass was water and the rock was the tip of a mountain protruding from the depths. Mommy used to play along when he was younger, but now she just laughed and smiled at his games. The pretzel was so good, but he wished he had some of that good gooey cheese to dip it in. That's when the man with the mask showed up.

He came from behind and put a cloth over Mommy's mouth. Her eyes went wide as she struggled. Milo dropped what was left of his pretzel. He watched in horror as Mommy fell asleep and toppled off the big rock. The man's mask was terrifying. It was made of pulled-tight leathery flesh sewn together with a collection of penises. They went in every direction, strung from the holes in their tips like Christmas garland wrapped around his fleshy head. Two green eyes peered out from a patchwork of mutilated sex organs with bulging veins and slithery foreskins.

Milo knew he should run. He knew he should fight. He knew he should do something, but he couldn't. It was just like school. When the other kids laughed at him and beat up him, made a spectacle out of him, he did nothing. He couldn't. He froze. He cried. He watched—just as he did now.

"Your turn," the man said. His cracked lips spoke through a visor of flaccid shafts, moving between an array of multicolored pubic hair that formed a crude goatee.

Milo started to cry, but he didn't budge. His eyes found his mother lying on the ground. Then, the clothed hand came over his mouth. His vision went funny, and he got tired quickly.

The next thing he knew, he was waking in the pit. The whole place had that smell like stepping in dog poop. There was a grating a few feet above them, and a ladder went up to the surface from there. Beside him, his mother was crying.

When Milo looked up, the man with the face of penises was staring down at them through the grate. He'd dragged a big hose down from above and put its end to the holes in the grate.

"What is that?" Milo asked nervously. "Mommy..."

His mother looked up. "It looks like a sewage pipe for a mobile home," she said. "A septic hose."

"Bingo," the cracked lips said between phalluses. He flicked a switch on the thick plastic hose, and a rush of brown sprayed out with incredible force. It burst through the grate and rained upon them. Milo was struck in the chest and launched backward by a forceful blast of what looked and smelled like diarrhea. It continued to pour on him aggressively like a firehose. He curled up on the ground while the filth painted him brown. It filled his ears and his eyes, his nose and his mouth. The man watched from above, his pink tongue lashing out and licking the penises that made up his face. He moaned as he stroked himself.

Milo choked and gagged, spit and wiped at himself, but it was pointless; more and more came until there was nothing left, and the plastic tube just drip, drip, dripped into the pit with them.

Then the man was gone.

Milo's mother crawled through the filth toward him on all fours. The shit squished between her fingers, caked under her nails, and squeezed between her toes. When she reached Milo, she scooped him up and held him between her legs to keep him in an upright sitting position. There was no water to be found, and she knew she couldn't leave him caked with putrid feces. She tried to wipe him clean, but her own filthy hands just smeared more shit onto his face. Milo felt sad because, through his red, burning, shit-covered eyes, he could see her crying.

"I'm sorry," he said, as if it were all his fault. Are you mad at me?"

"No baby, no," she said. "I'm going to take care of you. It's going to be alright."

Mommy sniffed back her tears. With no other options, she did what was necessary to clean her son and keep him from getting infected by the bacteria. She leaned forward and started licking the shit from his face. It was thick, and she gagged, but she didn't quit on him. She turned her head and spat out the chunky, brown liquid. Then she turned back to lick some more. The texture was sickening. Some grainy bits felt rough on her tongue, like licking sand, and other spots felt like congealed pudding.

She cleaned his eyes, his cheeks, his neck. She scooped the shit out of his ears with her tongue, coughing and spewing it out immediately. She groaned and fought the urge to vomit so she could keep going. She put her mouth over his nose and sucked the shit and snot out of his caked-up nostrils. That was the final straw, and she turned and vomited. Puke, shit, and snot all rained from her.

"Are you okay, Mommy?" he asked.

"I'm okay," she told him. "We just need to figure out how to get out of here. Are you okay?"

"I'm okay."

That was three days ago. Now, here they were, still trapped, still coated in filth and grime. Once a day, he would let water run down so they could catch it in their mouths. It seemed he didn't want them to die, or at least not quickly anyway. Milo watched as his mother pried a skull off of one of the bodies. She removed the cap, and sludge poured out, liquified brains. "Come on. You get one, too."

Milo listened, but he had trouble pulling the heads off the corpses. It wasn't as easy as it seemed. His mother got frustrated and came over to help. They pulled more heads off, ripped the remaining flesh from the bones, and did their best to pour out the contents.

The man came back. His tongue grazed the genitals as he spoke, "Drink."

He turned the hose on. Milo watched as Mommy hurried to fill all the skulls they'd acquired before the penis man took the water away. Milo opened his mouth and drank from the hose. He wanted to help, but he was so thirsty. Everything was so gross and terrible. He closed his eyes, tilted his head back, and tasted the freshwater that fell into his open mouth.

Then, the taste changed. It became salty and sour, sickening. Milo opened his eyes and saw the penis man urinating through the grate directly into his mouth. It was a reminder that he had more penises than the ones on his face—a lesson Milo would be sure to remember.

As Milo spat and gagged, the man left. His mother went to him. "I filled them all," she said. "We have water now. We can wash, drink—whatever we need. We changed the rules."

"But, Mommy, why are there so many dead people?"

Mommy looked sad. She went to a body and moved it into view. "See the shape of the hips. This was female." Then she went to another. "This one is small—a child, probably younger than you, even."

Milo felt terrified. "What are you saying?"

"They're mothers and children, Milo. They're just like us."

"They didn't make it out," he said, his lip quivering. "Are we going to die down here, too? Are we going to die, Mommy? I don't want to be like them—to be part of the mess for the next person. I can't."

His mother touched his face with both hands. "We're not going to. We're not. You hear me? We're not."

"Okay," Milo said but knew it was just like the "okay" he had given his father three days ago. He didn't believe what she said. He just knew what she wanted to hear. He was sure they would eventually be numbered among the pile of corpses.

His eyes roamed the root-entwined dirt walls, and he wondered how many more bodies were buried within. How many more dead were down here that they couldn't see? Milo felt like the entire ground was full of the dead—like they were surrounded. His eyes focused on the worms and beetles scurrying from dead ears, mouths, nostrils, and eyelids as he scanned the area. He imagined that he was one of the bodies, and the worms and insects were crawling over and out of him. There was someone else there, someone he couldn't see, someone who was disgusted by the sight of him.

"We're going to get out of here," Mommy said, "For now, try to get some rest."

Milo scoffed at this. *Rest...* How could anyone rest down here? They had to try to sleep sitting up, leaning against walls they now knew contained the dead. They couldn't lay down because the shit-water was too deep. They would drown in diarrhea and never wake up.

Milo hadn't slept in three days—not really. His mother managed, somehow. He couldn't figure it out. Maybe she was so exhausted or so sad or both. He watched her sit on a corpse and lean back against the dirt wall. Her eyes closed, and soon, she was snoring.

Milo watched a spider crawl onto his mother's face from the dirt wall. Before his very eyes, something that looked far too large to do so squeezed into her right nostril and disappeared. Milo waited, watching her to see if it came back out, but he saw no sign of the arachnid. Then it came up over her tongue and crawled out over her lip.

Milo gasped. He felt like someone was staring at him, and he turned around. No one was there, so he looked up. Those piercing eyes stared from between flaccid cocks. "What do you want?" Milo called to him, braver than usual.

The penises moved and stretched with squishing sounds to make way for the smile of the man who wore them. "Eat," he said.

Milo said a curse word he'd never said before and grabbed one of the skulls. He dumped the water out and used it to catch the cubes of meat falling through the grate. He ran around, moving left and right, splashing in the shit water as he went. Some of it splashed up into the skull, but he figured it was still better than if the meat had fallen in and been completely submerged. One piece of meat smacked him on the forehead and ricocheted into the filth with a splash.

When the man was gone, Milo ran to his mother. "Wake up, Mommy. I have food. I caught it for you."

His mother stirred. She coughed and groaned. Her skin was starting to look wrong—gray. He feared she was sick. He wouldn't know what to do if she got sick. Milo had just started fourth grade a few months ago. He wouldn't even know where to begin, trying to save a sick woman in a pit in the earth. "Please eat."

Her squinted eyes peered at him. She said hoarsely, "You eat first. I'll eat what's left."

Milo looked at the grayish-green meat in the skull and shook his head. "I'm young and healthy. It's okay. I'll eat next time, I promise."

He could tell she wanted to argue, but she nodded instead. Her fingers dug into the skull and came out with the meat. Maggots writhed within like they were trying to escape. It made Milo feel small—kin to the creatures. He watched his mother chew, gag, and chew some more. He watched the larvae break free of their rotten meat casing to scale her teeth and wriggle along her gums. Some climbed up her lips and toppled over the edge onto her shirt.

"I have to go to the bathroom," Milo said. "It's been three days. I can't hold it anymore."

"Then go," she said, chewing through the maggots and rotten meat.

"Where?"

"Anywhere. This whole fucking place is a toilet, Milo."

"But what will I wipe with?"

"I don't know. I'm sorry. Find something."

Milo frowned. He left her to eat and walked the pit looking for something he could use. Everything was already doused in the filth they waded through daily—everything except one dead child who'd fallen from the crumbling wall. Most of the boy was in the shitty liquid, but his head was out of it, leaning against the dirt. Milo stared at him for a moment. He must have been more recent than some of the others. He still looked like a boy, not a zombie or a skeleton. Milo touched his face. It was rough and leathery instead of soft like his own. Cringing, Milo used his fingernails to pick at the tough skin of the dead boy. It came free by his ear, peeled off like wrapping paper hiding a skull present.

Satisfied, Milo squatted over the shit and corpse pile, and what came out was pure liquid. It sprayed from him like a septic hose. He was sweating and feeling nauseous, struggling not to fall into the mess as it shot from him and spattered the bodies around him. He sprayed the walls and added to the murky depths of their pit.

Milo shook and swayed when he was finished, feeling horrible. He reached behind him without looking and grabbed the dead boy's face where it had peeled by his ear. It made a ripping sound as he tore it away. It kept coming. When it finally came free, Milo looked at it.

It was strange and surreal. Somehow, it still looked like a face, but it also looked like paper or leather, like the purse his mother always carried around. "I'm sorry," Milo said to the dead boy's severed face dangling from his fingertips. Then he reached back and used it to wipe the diarrhea from his bottom. He wanted to be completely clean, so he dug in deep. He could feel the boy's nose push into his rectum, and he held it there a moment, wriggled it, and then tugged it free. Panting, he dropped the shit-covered boy's face into the murk and tugged his pants up.

He heard the footsteps on the grate above them no sooner than he sinched them tight. Milo hurried over to his mother. Together, they looked up to see the penis man. He smiled at them, his fingers gently caressing the cocks covering his face, tracing the contours of their veiny girth. There was a sack with him. It was moving about atop the grate. When his thick fingers stopped with the penises, they went to the sack. He untied it, reached in, and pulled out a cat by scruff of the neck. It was two shades of orange and fighting to get free. "I'm giving this to you," the man said. "You can pet it and use it for the company or eat it. The choice is yours."

The man pulled a key from his pocket. Milo gasped at the sight of it. His mother was staring. The man used the key to open a door in the grate. As soon as he did, Mommy sprang forward, grabbed a handful of filth, and threw it through the opening. It hit the man in the face, and he cursed and lost his grip on the cat. The feline sought vengeance and clawed viciously at him. It clawed a penis free from his mask, which toppled into the filth, exposing a section of the man's face. His hand flew up to cover it, and he dropped the key. Milo's eyes widened as Mommy darted forward and caught it, laughing maniacally as she did. The man kicked the cat. It yelped and fell through the hole but held on with its paws, hanging from the grate. Milo watched in horror as the man stomped on its little furry cat hands until it let go with a squeal and fell into the brown sauce they lived in.

The man used one hand to cover the open space in his mask and the other to pull a gun from his waist. "Throw the key back up. Now."

"Go to hell," Mommy said.

"I will shoot you and your son."

Milo pulled the soaking wet, stinking cat and its broken paws from the filth with his eyes on his mother. She held the key out before the man who pointed his gun at her. He did something to make it click, and Milo knew it was a threat. He couldn't breathe. Mommy quickly shoved the key in her mouth and swallowed hard. Milo gasped.

"Fine," the man said. Then there was a bang, and Mommy's head exploded. Pieces of her once beautiful face went in every direction. Bone fragments scattered, and pieces of her brain matter rained down on Milo and the cat in his arms.

Milo was soaked in blood and covered in his mother's brains, holding a broken, whining cat streaked with shit and blood, and he rocked back and forth, staring at his mother's headless corpse as it sank into the muck. "Mommy," he said quietly. "Mommy?" Then he got louder until he started screaming, "Mommy! Mommy!"

As Milo screamed for his mother, who would never again answer, petting a cat no better off than he was, the man left. It took minutes for Milo to find the ability to move. He set the cat down atop the pile of bodies to remain dry and went to where he had last seen his mother. "Mommy?" he asked again more quietly.

His hands plunged into the filth in search of her. He felt around until his fingers grasped the broken skull where her face used to be. He cried out and retracted his hands.

Then he heard footsteps on the grate again. When he looked up, he saw the man staring down at him, his face turned so the exposed part wouldn't show. He dangled another key. "I had a backup," he said.

Milo watched in horror as he locked the grate again and left. Milo leaned against the wall and cried. The cat mewed, harmonizing with his agony.

As the hours passed, and Milo's sadness evolved into shock and depression, his stomach begged for food. After what his stomach had already done to him, he couldn't understand how it could possibly be hungry. The skull of meat was gone. He drank water from one of the other skulls and set another by the cat.

The cat... Milo looked at the poor, broken animal and wondered if he could actually do what the man proposed. The cat looked back at him. Milo shook his head. He couldn't do it, and he knew it. But he had to do something.

Swallowing the lump in his throat, Milo went forward. Cringing and wincing, he saw no other option. He dove into the shit swamp, fishing about with his hands for what he sought. Keeping his eyes shut, afraid of what the filth would do to them, he submerged himself as deep as he could. Finally, his hand grasped it, and he swam up, breaking the surface and gasping for air.

Carrying the penis with him, he went and sat on the pile of the dead beside the cat. The animal leaned over and started cleaning him much like his mother did, licking the shit from his face. "Thank you," Milo told the animal. "I'm so sorry he hurt you."

He raised the penis. "I have this. It's food. I'll share it with you." He leaned over to the back of the pile and wiped it on the skull of the now faceless dead boy to try to remove as much of the filth as he could. Then he sat forward and took a bite out of the black and purple helmet of the thing. It was tough, but he gnawed at it, chewing through. Then he ripped a piece of meat from the shaft and held it in his palm for the cat. The animal leaned over and nibbled at it, purring with contentment.

They went bite for bite until the entire penis was gone. Milo had considered saving some for later but was afraid it would end up filthy and make them sick. He didn't plan on being there another day anyway. He knew what he had to do; he had to get the key that was inside his mother.

Milo sat and petted the cat for a while to steel his nerves. Then, he knew he'd waited long enough. He would die down here if he didn't do this. Milo had spent enough of his life being forced around by the will of other people—bigger, stronger people. It was time for him to listen to his father and stand up for himself. With a deep breath, he slid into the surrounding liquid. Some of the bodies slid with him, disappearing beneath the surface.

Milo looked back and swallowed a lump in his throat. The cat looked at him curiously but then curled into a ball and closed its eyes. Apparently, cats were much better at dealing with these kinds of circumstances than people.

Milo went to where he had put his fingers in his mother's shattered head. He trembled and felt like he was going to throw up, but he reached into the liquid shit and fished for what was left of her. His fingers traced the lines and contours of her shattered skull and neck stump. Though he trembled with revulsion, Milo grabbed hold and dragged her. He pulled and pulled until her corpse rose from the foul, stinking liquid. Then, he dragged her up the pile of bodies and lay her to rest next to the cat. The animal looked at the newcomer indifferently, turned in a circle, and lay back down.

Milo panted with exhaustion, looking at what was left of his mother and lacking the tears to cry. He didn't know why. This was when he knew he should be crying, but all his tears were gone. Maybe it was that this headless thing no longer resembled his Mommy.

Milo wondered where the key would be. He felt her throat for lumps. It just felt like a throat to him, and he frowned again. Perhaps it had gone down and was in her stomach. He didn't know where the stomach was but would have to find it.

Milo had nothing sharp and doubted the cat would agree to help him. He traced his fingertips over his mother's belly. First, he pushed on it. Then he punched at it as his frustration grew. Human bodies couldn't be broken into so easily.

He thought about it, trying to figure out if there was another way. The body had openings. Mommy had a vagina, and it was big enough for him to have come out of as a baby. It would surely be a doorway into her, but what if the key fell out already? If a baby could come out, surely a key could, too. He felt perplexed. There was an opening in the butt where the poop came out, but when he stuck some fingers in there, he found it tight and hard to get much further. Frowning, he tried the vagina. Milo stuck his hand inside and then his wrist. He kept going, his whole arm pushing inside his mother's body. He couldn't feel anything that resembled a key. Maybe he couldn't get to the stomach that way. Maybe there were walls. He did feel bones at the top.

He cried out in frustration, which earned him a look from the cat. "I don't know how to do this?" Milo said to the animal. "I don't know where the key is."

The cat obviously didn't have the answers because it just closed its eyes and tightened the ball it was in.

Milo cringed. His arms and hands were already wet with his mother's juices, but he needed to find the key. He reached up to her top, where only her lower jaw and tongue remained. Swallowing again, Milo stuck his hand into her exposed throat. Her neck swelled oddly around his hand. He pushed further still. The body made odd noises, squishy and gassy sounds. The opening became tighter and more obstructed until he couldn't go any further. It was another dead end, and he was still keyless.

Milo cried out, trying to pull his arm back out. It wouldn't budge. He tried harder, and it remained stuck. Milo screamed as he yanked his arm back and forth. His mother's corpse swung with him like he had a person for an arm, connected by her misshapen, bulging throat.

Milo tried to get his feet into it, pushing on his Mommy's shoulders with his heels while trying to pull his arm back. Finally, his hand came free with a pop and splash of disgusting blood and bile. Mommy's body slid back into the murk.

Milo screamed and punched bodies and dirt. He started picking things up, throwing them, and yelling. The cat got up and moved away before lying back down to watch him carefully and lick its wounded paws.

Panting with frustration and exhaustion in equal measure, Milo dove back into the filth and retrieved his mother's body once again. He was angry and full of adrenaline, and this time, he pulled her right out and threw her on top of the pile with a roar. He had to get that stupid key so he could get out of this filthy, disgusting place. Milo dove onto his mother and sank his teeth into her belly. He gnashed at her flesh—ripped and tore, shaking his head like a dog. He didn't eat what he bit but spit it into his hand and offered it to the cat. The feline didn't seem to be interested. Maybe it was still full after the cock they'd devoured together.

Once her belly was slightly open, Milo dug his fingers into the small hole. He pulled and ripped at it savagely and worked tirelessly, screaming as he went. He tore his mother wide open and opened her further still. Then he plunged his hands into the mess of her and let his fingers swim through her blood and innards. He found different things, weird shapes, like leathery beans, and he pulled them free.

He ripped them open and tried to see what was in them. If they were empty or only full of blood, he tossed them into the filth and dove back in for more. Still no key.

His screams grew louder, and his frustration grew larger. That damned key had to be in her somewhere. It had to be. There was something in her, something long that he found coiled like a rope. He pulled it out, and it just kept on coming. He pulled and pulled, tugging the rope from his mother's corpse under the scrutiny of the cat. Milo bit into the rope and tore at it. It was stretchy and gummy—hard to puncture. But he was so enraged he got through it. Shreds of entrails were tossed in every direction.

Then it was there. About six feet in, he saw it glint in the light. Milo laughed like a crazy person and hurried to grab it. When the key was in his hand, he let his mother's ropes fall into the liquid shit at his feet. He held the key up, stared at it, and laughed some more.

"Time to go home," he said to the cat.

Milo grabbed the bodies and dragged them over to drop them under the grate. He worked tirelessly to move the entire pile. When he felt it was high enough, he climbed the dead and reached his thin arm through one of the holes in the grate. He stuck the key in the lock from the top and turned it even though the awkward angle hurt his wrist. Then he pulled his arm back and pushed the grate from underneath. It opened, and he whooped with excitement. The cat jumped up onto the pile of the dead, then jumped right past him through the opening. Its injured paws weren't broken after all. Cats were resilient, it seemed.

Milo pulled himself up. He climbed the ladder and reached a lid. It was dark and looked like a mountain. His heart was racing and pounding like a drum. He threw his weight into the lid, and the mountain toppled. When it did, he crawled free and got to his feet. He trembled. The cat hopped out and ran away. It stopped in the grass and looked back as if asking him to follow. When he didn't, it turned and ran on.

Milo was in shock. He was in his own yard. The lid he had pushed off was a fake rock that had always been there. He never knew what was under it. This didn't make any sense.

Milo stood and crossed the yard to the house. The back door was unlocked, so he went in. There was a time when his mother would have yelled at him for tracking mud into the house. He thought about that now and laughed. His mother was mud now.

He walked through the kitchen and down the hall to the living room. When he entered the living room, his father was sitting in his favorite recliner, sipping a beer and watching TV. Milo walked over and stood there, dripping mud, shit, and his mother's blood onto the carpet.

His father turned to look at him, and his eyes widened joyfully. His mouth echoed the sentiment with a giant smile. "My boy! You made it!" he said. "I'm so proud of you. Don't you see!" He jumped up from the recliner and hurried over to embrace his filthy son. "I knew you had it in you. I knew you were stronger than you realized. Now, no one will ever pick on you again, not after what you have endured and survived."

"Daddy?" Milo said quietly. "You did this?"

He looked at the end table next to the recliner and saw the mask of sewn penises. "Where did you get that?" Milo asked, pointing at the disgusting thing the man wore when he looked down on them in their pit. "Who did those belong to?"

"None of that matters," his father said, lovingly running his fingers through Milo's filth-matted hair. "What matters is you got out. You did. No one saved you. No one did it for you. You did it for yourself."

"That's what all of this was about? You did this for me?"

"Of course I did. You're my boy, and I love you."

"You killed Mommy."

"I killed many Mommies. I'm sorry, though. I know you'll miss her."

"Al those bodies...the women and children in there..."

"All mine," Daddy said. "Hard way to find out you have siblings, I know. But they were weak, Milo. They couldn't do what you did. If they had, they'd be here."

"Will you do it again?"

"With your next Mommy? Maybe. It depends on whether or not we have another child. I don't need another child now that I have you and finally have my success story. I'm getting older, but you never know, right? Love makes people do crazy things. We'll just have to see what happens."

Milo didn't respond. It was so much to wrap his head around. It didn't make sense to him. He felt crazy, like the world had broken, like his mind had broken. What was once real wasn't real anymore. He didn't know what to do with these new truths. He didn't know what to do with himself.

"Well, go upstairs and shower," Daddy said. "Get yourself cleaned up and put on some clean clothes. You've earned it. When you get done, we'll go to IHOP and get you some of those pancakes you like. I bet you're hungry, my boy—my good, good boy."

Milo stood there for a moment, staring at this man. How could this be his father? He still sounded like his father and acted like his father. The love seemed genuine, just as it always had, but how could that man be the man who killed his mother, pissed in his mouth, and kept him in a vat of shit hundreds of feet below the fake rock in the yard? The two things didn't fit together in his brain.

"Go on now," Daddy said. "This is the first day of the rest of your life, Milo. You're going to be great. Your life is going to be great. God, I'm so proud of you." Milo remained as he was. His father hugged him again, squeezed tightly with a contented groan, and then released him with a pat on the rear. "Maybe we'll go to the park after we eat or go to the store and pick out a toy or something. We'll figure it out. This is a great day, Milo!"

Milo turned and walked up the stairs without knowing what else to do. He needed to get out of these wet, heavy clothes and get the filth and grime off his flesh. It would probably take a hundred showers to truly get it all and remove the stench from his nose. At least he had gotten out, though. He was free.

Milo thought about the man waiting downstairs for him and wondered if that were true. He got out of that pit but only to move into the house of the man who put him there, the man he'd lived with his entire life thus far, the man who killed his mother. He was far from free. Milo climbed into the bathtub, under the shower spray, and sat down. He held his knees to his chest as the water beat down on him. Downstairs, he could hear his father singing.

Scalped Soup
By Carietta Dorsch

In the forest of Blue Ridge near Spruce Pine, there lived a man named Thomas. He chose a life of solitude, far away from society's prying eyes and judgmental whispers. Once a train conductor, Thomas had become a recluse, living off the land, disconnected from the modern world he despised so vehemently. He had built himself a small cabin hidden among the trees.

Thomas's hatred for people ran deep within his veins. He was scarred by the cruelty and deceit he'd witnessed throughout his life and despised the very essence of humanity. The thought of mingling with others, engaging in slothful conversations, or being subjected to their fault-finding gazes made his blood boil with rage. He had become a predator, lurking in the forest's shadows, waiting for unsuspecting trespassers to stumble upon his territory.

His heart raced with excitement whenever he sensed an intruder approaching. It was as if a hibernating monster within him awakened, craving the thrill of the hunt every time he heard the noise of a potential kill. Thomas had honed his survival skills over the years, becoming an expert in tracking, trapping, and killing. He relished the challenge of outsmarting his prey, his mind calculating every move and step as he prepared to strike.

His prey had been deer, squirrels, vultures, and even a dog. Once, he tried to battle with a bear but lost the fight in little to no time. But, the thing he loved most of all, above the hunt and the kill, was to eat the maggots that would appear on their decaying corpses.

After a few hours, the flies would head for the eyes, nose, and mouth and lay their eggs—and then he would wait. About two days after the eggs were planted, the larvae would usually hatch, and he'd let them feed for a little while to get plump for eating.

It all began one day while hunting a rabbit. He stumbled on a decaying skull near the creek bed where he washed his clothes. The sight of the maggots feasting upon the remnants of life within the skull ignited a perverse curiosity within him.

While most people would cringe at the thought of eating maggots, Thomas believed they were the finest delicacy the world had to offer. To him, maggots were the rice of the forest, and he would harvest them every chance he could.

Thomas spent years perfecting his technique for finding the juiciest and most succulent maggots. He would venture deep into the forest, armed with nothing but a hacksaw, a Bowie knife, a compass, and a keen eye. With each step, he would scan the ground, searching for any signs. The circling of vultures or buzzards would give an idea of where to look. The stench of decay was easy for him to sniff out like a police search dog.

On the days he couldn't find any, he would go hunting. He'd kill any animal that crossed his path, skin them, cut into their skull, and lay out their head as he would if they were bowls being placed on a dinner table.

Thomas was on his usual hunt when he came across a clearing where vultures were circling. The air was thick with the smell of decay. It had been a few days since his last bowl of maggots, and his mouth watered at the thought. He approached the rotting corpse of a deer, and to his astonishment, the stomach was spread open from another animal's feeding. The carcass was filled with an abundance of maggots. They squirmed and wiggled, covering every inch of the intestines.

Thomas's eyes widened with delight, and he couldn't believe his luck. It was a feast beyond his stomach's hunger. He chuckled, knowing he would have plenty to save for later.

Without hesitating, Thomas knelt and began collecting the maggots, his hands moving swiftly and expertly. He could already taste their deliciousness, imagining the savory flavor that would soon grace his palate. He shoved a handful into his mouth and basked in the feeling of them twisting on his tongue before starting to chew.

As his teeth came down, he felt their juices explode onto the roof of his mouth. Their bodies crunched and released the savory liquid he sought day in and day out. He chewed, and swallowed, and then repeated the process.

He greedily ate a few more handfuls, then scooped them up and thrust them into his pockets. Maggots fell from the overflowing pockets of his jacket and pants before he realized he couldn't carry any more on his person. He retrieved his hacksaw from its homemade holster on his belt and began to saw the deer's neck.

As he hacked into the bone with one hand, he pulled and jerked with his other until, finally, the head came off. Then, he packed the maggots into the neck and mouth of the deer like clothes in a suitcase. Satisfied with the amount, he began his trek back to his cabin.

Inside the cabin, a man lay on a rickety bed. He had been injured by one of Thomas' booby traps. His shin bone protruded through a deep gash on his leg that refused to heal. The wound had become an infected breeding ground for something far more sinister.

Thomas watched the man's eyes widen as he entered with the deer head. The man jerked against his restraints as Thomas walked by, gazing at his wound. Duct tape stifled his voice as he tried to scream.

Thomas placed the deer head and all his findings on the table next to his copy of *Finn's Adventure* by Crystal Baynam. The sight of the man struggling against the rope restraints made him smile. He felt good about the day as he walked to the bed and looked at the man's leg.

Hands trembling with anticipation, Thomas reached down to inspect the wound. What he saw made his lips turn upward. Maggots, nearly a hundred of them, wriggled and squirmed inside the bloody crater. Their pale bodies glistened in the dim light of the lantern, their tiny mouths devouring his flesh.

Sweat beaded down the man's face. His body convulsed, and his screams of agony vibrated quietly through the duct tape. His expression of horror was unlike anything Thomas had ever seen. He could tell the man wanted to be put out of his misery. The man's wound had become a farm to feed Thomas' twisted appetite.

In his hand, Thomas gripped a knife, its blade coated with dried flakes of skin from previous victims. The man before him gasped for breath, his face contorted in terror, as his life force slowly drained away with each passing moment. Snot ran from the man's nose, coating his upper lip in thick yellowish mucus that had built up around the duct tape like icing on a cake. His tears trickled in rapid waterfalls down his cheeks as Thomas cut into him, slowly twisting the blade and widening the wound in his leg.

Blood spewed from the cut, a grisly fountain that seemed to defy gravity before flowing to the cabin floor. Thomas licked his lips as a splash of blood hit his mouth. Each drop landed with a sickening patter, staining the wood a deep, haunting crimson.

The man's body shook violently, and his breathing became a series of frantic pants through his nose. His moans were labored, and his struggling weakened as Thomas relentlessly wiggled the blade.

Thomas's heart raced with a mixture of exhilaration, emotional arousal, and madness as he felt the warm stickiness between his fingers. The sensation sent pleasurable shivers down his spine, a twisted joyfulness that fueled his insatiable hunger for more. The knife's handle was drenched in the man's life essence.

As the man's body crumpled to the cabin floor, his blood puddled around him, seeping from the wound at an alarming rate. It spread like a sinister shadow, creeping between the floorboards and staining everything it touched.

As Thomas hovered over him, eyes fixated on the open wound, the wind carried a mournful howl. Thomas reached down and picked up a blood-soaked maggot. He held it between his fingers and admired it briefly before placing it on his tongue, savoring the flavor before chewing and swallowing his treat.

The forest was enchanting, with fall-colored trees and chirping birds. Erica and Jerry followed a narrow trail, their footsteps muffled by the soft carpet of fallen leaves. The silence was broken only by the occasional rustling of small animals scurrying away.

They stumbled upon a small clearing as the sun reached its highest point. In the center stood an ancient oak tree, its branches reaching toward the sky like gnarled fingers.

Jerry paused to admire a cluster of wildflowers while Erica leaned in to smell their sweet fragrance.

"Today is such a beautiful day," Erica said.

"Oh gosh, yes. It's gorgeous out here," Jerry said. "I've never been hiking before."

"What?" she asked, surprised. "But you are such an outdoorsy person."

"Yeah, farms and horses, but not woods and trees," he replied.

"Well, we'll have to do this more often then."

"Yes, we do," he said as he pulled her close and gave her a quick kiss.

As they continued their hike, they came to another clearing with a lush garden of tomatoes and what looked like potatoes.

"Wow, look at this," Jerry said.

"Does someone live out here, you think? It's pretty far from the city," Erica said with a hint of concern.

"Nah, I don't think so. It looks to be natural. There are no rows or fences. I mean, there's not even a scarecrow. Whoever made this is long gone. It was probably homeless guys or hippies or some kid practicing his green thumb so he could grow weed."

After five minutes of walking away from the crops, Erica and Jerry noticed the sunlight struggling to penetrate the thick canopy. They saw an old cabin. Its weathered wooden exterior, worn by time and the elements, blended seamlessly with the surrounding wilderness. The cabin's presence was perplexing and concerning, catching the attention of Erica and Jerry in different ways.

Jerry felt curious as they approached the cabin, while Erica seemed anxious. The structure stood nestled within a sea of emerald green foliage. The air was heavy with the scent of damp earth and decaying leaves.

"Should we go in?" Jerry asked.

"This could be someone's home."

"Erica," Jerry began explaining, "look at this place. It's dusty, broken, rotting, and obviously abandoned. Come on, babe. It'll only take a second or two."

"Okay," she said reluctantly.

They cautiously stepped onto the creaking porch, their eyes scanning the exterior. The logs used to build the walls had rotted in multiple places, and the steps were made of different varieties of wood, creating a patchwork of muted colors. The planks beneath their feet groaned in protest. Though the windows were adorned with cobwebs and hinted that any resident was long gone, Erica frowned.

"Look at this place. No one has been here in a long time," Jerry said reassuringly.

"I hope you're right."

Pushing on the heavy door, they were greeted by resistance. The door was locked. Jerry tried again, but the door didn't give.

"What the hell. This is a bummer."

"It's probably for the best. Let's go."

"Come on, Erica. Stop being such a downer."

Jerry went to the window and looked in. He could see dust particles dancing in the air. The room was sparsely furnished, with a worn-out armchair and a small wooden table covered in dust. The remnants of a fireplace stood in the center.

"Come on, Jerry. I want to get back home before dark."

"Okay, Erica," he said, his annoyance undisguised. Let's get the hell outta here."

"Thank you," she said, her sarcasm unnoticed by Jerry.

Close by, Thomas heard the couple while chopping wood for his stove. He hid behind a thick oak. His eyes darted back and forth, fixating on the unsuspecting couple just a few yards away. He watched them intently and couldn't help but smile at the thought of how many nests they could provide for his darling maggots.

As the couple walked deeper into the forest, the man's grip tightened around his axe's smooth, wooden handle. His fingers trembled with a mix of excitement and hunger. His senses heightened to every rustle of leaves and snap of twigs. He knew one wrong move could shatter his ability to stay hidden, but he also needed to know where they were.

With a nimble and soundless movement, he emerged from the shadows of the oaks, his eyes gleaming with a sinister spark. He watched Jerry's expression turn from curiosity to sheer panic at his sudden appearance. As Thomas swung the axe, the blade sliced through the air, finding its mark with a sickening wet SHUSH. Jerry crumpled to the forest floor, grasping his neck to stop the outpour of blood. His body twitched, and his legs jerked like fish out of water.

Thomas gave the axe another hard swing, and Jerry's head rolled off to the side of the blade as it became disconnected from his body. When Thomas removed the axe, a geyser of blood erupted from Jerry's neck and coated the forest floor.

Erica's scream sounded like a lone coyote on a full moon, her eyes wide at the sight of her husband trying to shove his blood back into his neck's gaping hole and then being decapitated. Thomas' gaze shifted to her, his lips curling into a yellow smile. He knew that his work had only just begun. He had to go the extra mile if he really wanted to have a feast.

Erica trembled in fear as Thomas slowly approached her. With each step he moved forward, she moved back until her muscles seemed to betray her. She stood frozen in place as Thomas stood in front of her.

He reached out, his fingers grazing her trembling cheek. "Don't worry," he whispered, his voice dripping with a chilling calmness. "You will serve a greater role. You will be their queen," he said, brushing her cheek again.

Erica took advantage of his distraction by forcefully kneeing him in the cock and shoving him away before darting off. She could feel her heart pounding in her chest as she ran deeper into the forest, desperately trying to escape this deranged woodsman. The wind whipped through the trees, causing the leaves to rustle and the branches to sway, making it hard for her to get a sense of direction. Every step she took echoed in the silence, betraying her location to the attacker following her.

As Erica darted between the trees, her breath came in ragged gasps, and her lungs burned. She spotted a road in the distance and made a desperate dash toward it. Her heart soared with hope as she imagined a car coming to her rescue.

Suddenly, her vision went black. Then, after what seemed like seconds, she slowly returned to consciousness. Her eyes fluttered before opening wide with fear. She was tied in a sitting position on an old, dirty mattress. She tugged at the ropes binding her wrists and pulled at the chains on her ankles that attached her to a dead man.

"You're finally awake," Thomas said as he rose from his chair and walked toward her.

He squatted in front of Erica, lifted the Bowie knife, and placed its blade on her skin. Its touch sent a shiver down her arm. The cold steel glided against her forearm, tracing a delicate line along her skin. The sound of the blade's soft whisper on her flesh was sickening to her ears.

Erica whimpered and tried to pull away. Her eyes brimmed with tears as she begged. "Please let me go. I promise I won't tell anyone anything. Please just let me go."

"You can't go anywhere. You have to serve them," he replied.

Thomas touched the blade's edge to her hairline, applied pressure, and watched as blood crept around the tip of the knife. As the incision deepened, his hands moved with the precision of a hunter. He carefully folded back the skin as it flapped open, then took hold of the flaps. A strange, sucking sound emanated as he peeled back the fleshy layers, exposing the bone beneath. Knowing it could only be done once, the sight was mesmerizing and sad. It was an unnatural ballet of flesh and bone fighting for his eyes' attention.

She screamed and tried to fight against the ropes, but the restraints held fast. Tears flowed down her cheeks as he worked. He remained unaffected as her screams turned into whimpering and tearful pleas for mercy.

Without hesitation, Thomas raised his hacksaw from its homemade holster and began to saw back and forth into Erica's skull. The saw's metal teeth biting bone filled the room with a gritty grinding sound and blended with her screams. Thomas's hands trembled with a mixture of lust and excitement as blood trickled down her face, mingling with her auburn locks. Her screams shifted to a high-pitched yodel as her voice began to give before finally softening to a wet and bubbly croak.

Thomas poked his fingers into her mouth and fish-hooked her cheek, pulling tight to get a better hold of her head. He couldn't resist and had to stop sawing to admire his work for a moment.

He continued to saw around her cranium in a jagged, square-like shape until he could get his fingers under the edge of her skull. Then, he pulled upward and lifted the ragged square off with a wet, plopping sound.

As Thomas peeled parts of her scalp away from the opening, he could see the delicate layers of skin and tissue. An intricate web of blood vessels and nerves pulsed beneath the gray film, and he could feel her struggle growing weaker.

Bubbles of red-tinted spit parted her lips, and she began to tremble. Just as Thomas' fingers were about to scoop into her brain like a salsa dip, he had an idea and pulled them back. He wanted to feed the maggots first. His fingers only grazed her exposed brain, but he looked down at the sound of her pissing herself when he did. He picked up a handful of maggots from the leg-hive of the dead man beside her and sprinkled them onto her brain like cheese on spaghetti.

Her body convulsed, and her arms thrashed about as the maggots began feeding on her gray matter. The smell of her urine and blood drove him over the edge. Thomas's hunger overcame him, and he couldn't resist the temptation any longer. He licked his lips and dove his fingers into her brain like a package of thawed hamburger, digging out a chunk.

Maggots clung to his moist fingers as he brought it to his watering mouth. With each scoop, Thomas tasted the tang of raw meat mingled with the crunch of maggots between his teeth in an instant burst of new flavor like nothing he'd ever experienced. Pleasure surged throughout his entire body.

As Thomas ate, he couldn't help but think he could have this more often if he moved back to the city. His mouth watered at the thought of being able to eat maggots and brain every night. He moaned in ecstasy as he chewed and reached for another fistful.

It was about time for a change of scenery after all, he thought, as he felt a maggot slide down his throat. Thomas rose with his hacksaw still in his hand and left the cabin. He stood outside for a moment, still savoring the taste of his scalped soup, before walking in the direction of town.

The Professional
by Stephen Cooper

Ethan was a professional, goddamn it, so the idea of being hired to take out some nobody irked him. With a one hundred percent success rate, he was the best hitman in the country. He was contracted to snuff out rival gang bosses, politicians who'd overstepped their station or cheated on their rich, vindictive wives, and witnesses in deep hiding who could bring down multi-billion-dollar corporations. They could hide from everyone else, but not Ethan Rage—he was that good.

He had a reputation for brutality as well.

You didn't pay Ethan to make it look like suicide, natural causes, or any of that other pussy shit. You hired Ethan to make a fucking statement—to make anyone else who'd considered crossing the line back the fuck down and beg for forgiveness, even if they were in the right.

Because if Ethan was coming after you, you were dead. One Hundred Percent guaranteed.

Have the success rate to prove it.

And it wouldn't be pleasant. It wouldn't be suffocated in your sleep or poisoned over a period of time. More likely, you'd be hung from your intestines and left to rot in your piss and shit or cut to shreds with some rusty chicken wire and fed to a pack of feral dogs... if you were lucky.

Ethan had a solid reputation. He was a man who got the job done—a man of high class, professional standards, and sadistic methods.

So why the fuck am I suddenly being asked to end some PE Teacher-looking motherfucker?

The mark had no gang affiliations, wasn't filthy rich, hadn't witnessed any nefarious crime, and appeared to have zero scandal attached to his name. You could pass him in the supermarket and think nothing of it. He didn't even have an aura about him.

A fucking nobody.

Ethan didn't have time for nobodies.

But money talked, and someone was paying him way too much green for the job. It was too much for him to say no, even if he did think the hit would hurt his street cred. He didn't want to be known as the assassin who killed Jerry the petrol station worker, *or whoever the fuck this blank was.*

Ethan wanted to be the guy who brought down barbaric regimes— who toppled notorious gangs—and killed smug-faced high-ranking public figures. *Not some douchebag in grey sweats.*

This Jerry-the-gas-station-working, PE-Teacher-looking motherfucker was called Bob, which seemed even blander to Ethan. And instead of pumping gas at the local Seven-Eleven, he was the manager of a furniture store.

It got worse...

He lived alone, didn't socialise, had a fucking dad bod, and wore thick-rimmed glasses when watching shitty reality shows. It would be the uncoolest hit of all time—like killing someone's stodgy uncle after they got laid off from their pathetic job and their overbearing ex-wife took what little they had left.

Ethan decided to forgo his usual flair, as he was already bored of the hit. Instead, he'd break into Bob's house, put a bullet in the back of his head, and maybe be home in time to watch the game. If not, he could watch it there and use Bob's rotting corpse as an ashtray while he smoked the evening away.

The instructions he'd been given were simple. Kill Bob. It sounded like the beginning of a joke, but that was it. Kill Bob. Ethan laughed at the mundane instruction but didn't laugh at the money on offer.

He didn't need the cash, but it was a bigger payday than when he'd stuffed a grenade down some minister's throat and exploded him in front of his young family. They'd died in the blast, too, which he promptly received a bonus for. *Plus, hazard pay for being in proximity of an explosion.*

Bob wasn't worth a hundredth of that paycheck, yet Ethan was getting double for him. *Why?*

Fuck it, he finally decided after staring at the offer.

He'd gone through Bob's file, and the only thing of note was he'd survived a car crash once, in which six other people brutally died, and he'd beaten cancer with zero treatment. That did seem pretty odd, but Ethan assumed the information was unreliable.

He had asked his employer, 'Why Bob?' and was told rumour had it Bob couldn't be killed. They wanted to find out if the rumour was true or not.

What horseshit.

And who the fuck pays millions to check the truth of a rumour? Couldn't they have just mowed the asshole down in their car or blown his fucking house up?

It all seemed ridiculous—childish even. But they paid half in advance, so who was Ethan to question it?

Although, he did question every single part of it. The guy had to be something to someone. Otherwise, none of it made a lick of sense. He supposed it didn't matter. Whatever the reason, Bob was as good as dead the moment Ethan signed the contract.

Ethan surveyed Bob's house and wasn't surprised to discover it was as vanilla as him. The whole bland neighbourhood looked like it was stuck in time—white picket fences and all that shit. Inside, the house was equally flavourless—white walls, beige carpet, grey suits in a generic IKEA wardrobe.

I'll be doing him a favour.

Ethan made himself a sandwich while he waited for Bob to return home. Ham and cheese, because God forbid the dull cunt have anything with a bit of zing to it in his fridge. He made himself a coffee, too, despite the only caffeine on offer being some store-brand instant shit.

Yep, he was going to shoot Bob out of pure principle.

He finished the unimaginative sandwich and dish-water coffee just as Bob returned home in his soccer-dad station wagon. *Typical.*

Bob was alone, as expected.

"Live alone, die alone," Ethan smirked to himself as he took a position in the living room, leaving the plate and cup on the kitchen side to wash up after he was done putting a bullet in Bob.

He may have been a ruthless killing machine, but he had manners and hated mess… despite how much he enjoyed creating it.

Bob was humming as he opened the door. It wasn't a song Ethan was familiar with. Instead, it sounded more like one of those pre-programmed tunes you got from a cheap, shitty keyboard.

More reason to off the cunt.

Ethan watched Bob slide off his brown loafers and walk into the living room none the wiser until Ethan stepped behind him with his pistol aimed at the back of Bob's head.

The silenced pistol barely made a whimper as the bullet tore through the back of Bob's cheap haircut and lodged itself into his mundane brain.

He fell to the floor, dead, probably completely unaware he'd even been shot. *Easy money.*

"Cancer zero, Ethan one," the ruthless hitman chuckled.

What a fucking joke, he thought, looking down at the dead fat body. "Can't be killed," he scoffed, giving the ample corpse a swift kick in the guts.

Ethan holstered his pistol and went back to the kitchen. While he didn't mind leaving a body lying around, he wasn't about to go without washing his cup and plate.

He ran the hot water and let his hand linger under the tap, feeling the freshness of the water splash against his skin until it started to burn. It was something he always did after a job. Usually, it would be the first stages of wiping the blood from his hands and ridding the gore from under his immaculate fingernails, but there was none of that today.

The kill was as uninspired as the man he murdered. *A dull day for a big paycheck.*

Ethan dunked the cup and plate under the water, scrubbing away the crumbs and coffee stains before returning both items to the cupboard. He shook his head at the monotonous assortment of typical mugs and characterless plates lining the shelves. Bob was better off dead, even if Ethan still had no clue why he was hired to kill the tedious man.

He replaced the bland tea towel over the rack and left the unimaginative kitchen, ready to head home and catch the game, when he noticed something missing from the living room.

Bob.

Bob's meaty paws wrapped around Ethan's unsuspecting face as he grabbed at him from behind.

His fingers began clawing Ethan's eyes while the hitman struggled to get a grip on the dangerous digits. He yanked one of Bob's fingers upwards as it poked against his eyeball and heard the finger snap, but Bob didn't relent. Instead, he doubled his efforts as his middle finger pressed against Ethan's right eye, desperate to pop the fucking thing.

Ethan could feel the pressure on his eyeball. It was ready to burst any moment. Composing himself like the pro he was, he twisted away from the claw-like grasp in a last-ditch effort to save the peeper. Bob's fingers fell from Ethan's eye but scratched the hitman from cheek to chin as he tore up the assassin's handsome features as a consultation prize.

Ethan head-butted Bob once his eye was safe, with the hardened blow creating further separation. He stepped forward and landed a stiff haymaker on Bob's chubby face, sending the man spinning. Then he followed with a rib cruncher to his stomach, but Bob remained upright.

The presumed dead man charged Ethan and buried his broad shoulder into the lean hitman. They crashed against the wall as they continued to trade blows—Bob from below, Ethan above.

Bob caught Ethan with a vicious uppercut to the throat, making the hitman gasp as he pounded on Bob's dumb face. Bob's eyes blackened, and his nose twisted from its original position as he reached for Ethan's holstered gun.

"No...you...don't..." Ethan wheezed, each word more painful than the last as his damaged eyes watered and his throat felt like a railroad spike had been shoved through it. He could feel skin hanging from his previously perfect face as well.

The wounded hitman drew the pistol first and shot the motherfucker all over again. The gun ignited four times, with each bullet planting itself into Bob's bloated stomach.

Blood exploded from each wound, soaking both men before Bob stumbled back and dropped to the floor. He clutched his guts as blood gushed, oozing through his fat fingers and staining his grey suit. The additional crimson was a welcome sight to Ethan as he tried to catch his breath and work out what the fuck just happened.

From his vantage point, he stared down at the dying man noting all the additional damage he'd caused to the bastard's face but was miffed by the absence of a fucking hole in his head.

Had he missed? From point-blank range?
Not a fucking chance.
But how else could the silly cunt be alive?

It didn't matter now. He'd just have to kill him a second time.

Ethan aimed the pistol at Bob and fired the last few bullets in the gun. There was no mistaking whether he was alive or not this time as blood jetted from the fatal wounds in the centre of Bob's fat, deformed head.

"Fuck," Ethan coughed, but the word failed to fully leave his mouth. Instead, he threw up beside the *once again* dead man. He held his throat and felt something jingling around inside as he wheezed. The bastard had caused some serious damage.

"Fuck," he tried saying again, at both the fight and the state he'd been left in.

He was still confused about how exactly he could have missed from point-blank range, but there weren't many explanations. Except...

... Maybe the gun hadn't fired?

After all, he had the silencer on, so he wouldn't have noticed the lack of a loud bang. If that was the case, someone was going to get a severe ass-whooping for selling him a defective weapon. That shit didn't fly in his world.

Ethan lowered himself to the floor to catch his breath. He stared at the gun like he was interrogating it. If it had misfired, it definitely hadn't the second time around. Odd, but the end result was what mattered: Bob was dead.

He looked at the bullet-ridden corpse. "Tougher... than... you... look," Ethan offered, already impatient with his fucked up throat. He wiped the blood from his face, being careful not to touch the peeled, stinging skin, and blinked his damaged eye a few times, glad the damn thing was still in its socket.

Bob had come dangerously close to bursting the fucking thing, and that would have been that. A one-eyed hitman was cool on the silver screen but was a career-ender for a man like Ethan. Not that he used guns often, but they were always there for backup.

Now, he needed to decide whether Bob was worthy of evisceration.

He hadn't considered him so beforehand, but it was extremely rare he had to kill someone twice. The only other time involved Ethan doing CPR on a cunty Lawyer so he could torture him some more. But this was the first time a corpse had got back up of its own accord and tried to scratch his fucking eyes out.

Yep... Bob was officially upgraded from 'one and done' to 'switch on the TV cos it's gonna be a long night.'

"Have. It. Your. Way. Bob. I'll. Rip. You. Apart." Ethan struggled to joke with the corpse. The words still hurt but were an improvement from a few minutes earlier. He hoped Bob had caused less damage than he first thought.

Ethan wasn't the only one on the mend as a bullet popped out of Bob's stomach.

"What. The. Fu..."

Ethan didn't even get to finish his sentence as a second bullet rolled from its former home inside of Bob to the blooded, formerly beige, *now red*, carpet beneath him.

The other two bullets quickly followed.

Was this some kind of release of gas type thing? Ethan speculated, having never heard of such bullshit in all his life. His brain was trying to devise some logical reason for the impossibility because he'd never seen anything like it, and he'd killed enough guys for it to have come up at some point.

Ethan instinctively took hold of Bob's wrist and checked the dead man's pulse.

Still dead.

"Where. Do. You. Keep. The. Tools?" Ethan mumbled in between a coughing fit, which made his damaged throat feel even worse and caused him to throw up for a second time.

Bob didn't answer as the hitman climbed back to his feet, wiping the drool from his mouth and blinking his eyes once again.

Boring Bob really had fucked him up.

Ethan left the living room searching for a toolbox but quickly poked his head around the door to check on Bob. He remained dead on the floor.

"Dumb cunt," Ethan directed at the corpse, readjusting his throat after each word. It hurt like hell, but he was beginning to think there wasn't any permanent damage when he got the words out in one go.

He searched a cupboard under the stairs and quickly found what he was looking for. Ethan dropped the metal toolbox down beside Bob, barely missing the puddle of puke and blood gathering beside the body. He rifled through the content until something caught his good eye.

Ethan yanked a hammer from the box, thinking he'd crack the asshole's skull open and find the rest of the bullets—maybe put them all together in a jar.

Some souvenirs of Bob's death.

He wasn't usually the sentimental type, but Bob's second wind impressed him, even if he thought it had little to do with the man himself. He wasn't 'un-killable,' just one of the luckiest son-of-a-bitches to ever live.

Past tense...

... It became present tense again when Bob reached into the toolbox, grabbed a screwdriver, and rammed it through Ethan's foot.

"Fuck!" The hitman screamed at the top of his lungs, more out of shock than from the searing pain in his foot. Whatever damage was starting to heal in his throat, he re-hurt with the scream.

"What... the... fuck?" he croaked at the reanimated corpse.

The bullets in Bob's forehead dropped from his skull. A hammer was no longer required to smash them out as they casually lay next to the other blunt escapees.

Bob yanked the screwdriver from Ethan's foot, taking his middle toe with it, leaving Ethan's left foot looking bird-like.

Ethan struggled to breathe as he brought the hammer he was still somehow holding down onto Bob's skull, compressing the top of the former dead man's head. He fell atop him, having put everything into the swing and not being used to the balance of having a fucking toe missing.

Both men lay together in a heap on the bloody living room carpet.

Time for round two... *or is it three?*

Bob jabbed the screwdriver at Ethan's side, but Ethan flinched away before it caused any real damage. It left a nasty scratch, though. In reply, Ethan viciously smashed the hammer against Bob's jaw. The weapon slipped from his grasp on the follow-through as the jaw hung loose.

"You can't kill me," Bob finally spoke, apparently waiting to have no fucking jaw left before opening his mouth for the first time.

Ethan was having none of that shit. He was a professional. If you hired him to kill someone, he killed them. And dad-bod-Bob was not going to be the fucking exception. Not a chance. No goddamn fucking way! Ethan had a reputation to uphold, and whatever unnatural mumbo-jumbo bullshit was going on with this freak, it wouldn't stop Ethan from completing his task.

He'd kill Bob as many times as it took.

Ethan hadn't thought to reload the pistol since the last time he killed the cunt, so he pistol-whipped the hell out of Bob instead. He caved in Bob's eyes, practically knocked what remained of his nose right off his broken face, bashed the impression in his skull deeper, and kept swinging until his hand began to tire.

Then he grabbed a second screwdriver from the toolbox and stabbed it through Bob's ribcage into his somehow beating heart.

The beats slowed to a stop as another fountain of blood sprayed from the dying organ, covering Ethan's face and stinging his peeled skin.

"What... the... fuck... Bob?" Ethan questioned in slow, laboured breaths like he'd just run a marathon. He stared down at the man he'd just killed for a third time with absolute disgust etched on his pained face. "What... the... fuck?" he silently screamed once more as he impaled the screwdriver into Bob's heart another sixteen times.

Bob didn't answer, mostly because he was dead.

But Ethan wasn't buying it this time round. *Fool me once and all that.*

Ethan pulled a saw from the toolbox. *You can't come back to life if you've got no head,* he reasoned and began hacking at Bob's neck almost on autopilot.

What a fucking ordeal. This had been the easiest job he'd ever had less than half an hour ago.

He tried not to look at his severed toe lying on the floor next to the body. Bob had ripped through his expensive shoes with the screwdriver and managed to deform his foot before he knew what was happening. One minute, he was dead. The next, he was mutilating Ethan.

He wanted to pick the toe up and put it on ice in case there was a chance of saving it, but he was reluctant to leave the body until he'd cut the bastard's head clean off.

What the actual fuck, he thought once more.

What was this bullshit?

He could barely reason away the phantom shot that hadn't killed the cunt the first time around, but there was no mistaking the second death. He put six bullets in him, two in his forehead. He'd checked the man's pulse. It wasn't light, or shallow, or faint, or any of those other bullshit phrases to make it sound like the man was still alive. There wasn't a fucking pulse. It was as simple as that.

Oh… and he had two fucking bullets in his fucking forehead.

Fuck!

Ethan couldn't stare at the runaway toe any longer and gingerly climbed to his feet, leaving the saw embedded in Bob's thick neck. He limped to the kitchen and filled a food bag with ice, praying the whole time that not only was his toe salvageable, but also Bob didn't get back up with a fucking saw dangling from his half-hacked grisly neck.

Returning to the living room, he was thankful to see the dead body still where he left it. He almost muttered the words aloud and probably would have if he'd been able.

He popped the loose toe into the ice bag but not before throwing up again when he saw the state of it. Ethan knew the likelihood of the severed toe being reattached was somewhere around the zero mark. He couldn't even shout in frustration as his throat felt messed up. His hand kept going to the great big gash on his side, too, adding to his injury woes, while he continued to resist the urge to pull the dangling skin from his cheek, which was practically burning at this point.

He'd thought Bob barely caught him with the attempted stab, but he mustn't have felt the pain as the adrenaline surged through his body while he fought off Zombie Bob, *or whatever the fuck he was.*

In actuality, Bob had caught him pretty good with the screwdriver.

Ethan wasn't convinced he wouldn't pass out from the various wounds, as embarrassing as the notion was.

Of all the targets...

'*Un-killable.*' It turned out they hadn't been joking.

They could have fucking warned him rather than being so vague about it. No wonder they hired him and hadn't just tried to run the fucker over as Ethan suggested.

Boring Bob. There was more to the sad sack of meat than met the eye.

There was definitely some lesson to be learnt here about not underestimating someone or judging a book by its cover or something, but Ethan had no time for that shit at the moment. He just wanted to make sure Bob couldn't make any more miraculous returns, then get his toe fixed and drink himself into a stupor for the rest of the week. *Maybe even take a vacation afterwards.*

With a few more hacks of the saw, Ethan hoped Bob would be *dead* dead... dead, and the whole nightmare would be over. He watched in relief as the head tumbled from Bob's shoulders when he drove the saw through the remaining meat and bone. A big part of him wanted to chop up the rest of the body, too, but he had nothing left.

His eye was still hurting and had gone bright red. His face was peeling, and his throat would need some fixing, while his side needed stitching up, and he had a toe to reattach. There wasn't time to chop Bob into itty-bitty pieces, even if the asshole deserved it.

Ethan was drenched in blood from his head to what remained of his toes. He'd parked his car a block away to avoid suspicion, expecting the job to be a quick in and out. The notion was almost laughable now that he'd killed the man three fucking times!

He couldn't leave the house like this and hadn't brought a spare set of clothes. Again, it was Bob. Fucking Bob! Why would he need anything to deal with such a nobody?

Ethan knew he'd have to have words with the rich fuck behind the contract. He had too many questions at this point, and the asshole might be the only one who knew the answers... unless Bob somehow found a way to reattach his head and come back to life.

There's a better chance of that than me getting my toe fixed.

Ethan shook his head at the thought. *Preposterous*, yet after what he'd already witnessed...

As much as it pissed him off, and as stupid as it would look, Ethan knew he'd have to borrow one of Bob's extra-large dull grey suits to get back to his car. Then he could drive home, change properly, and contact the sawbones. He hoped his on-call Doc didn't ask too many questions.

He shouldn't; he was paid handsomely not to.

Ethan had no idea how he'd explain bland Bob and his bullet-sponge head, nor did he want to. He knew if anyone told him the same story, he wouldn't believe them.

Washing up the cup and plate without a lick of blood on him felt like a distant memory. He decided a quick shower was in order, then a change of clothes. Maybe he'd feel mildly better after.

As he began to peel off his shirt, he swore Bob's head rolled towards his body. Normally, he'd dismissed the idea immediately, but he'd seen things now. He had the injuries to prove where that sort of denial got him.

So, instead, he stared at the head, waiting to see if it would do something.

And it fucking did...

Ethan went bug-eyed as he watched Bob's decapitated head roll across the splatter-stained carpet back towards the shoulders it once sat on.

I'm going crazy. It's the only reasonable explanation.

He gathered his belongings and hobbled to the front door, noping the fuck out. Enough was enough. This was madness. Utter madness. He'd cut the guy's fucking head off, and he still wasn't dead. If it worked on a *Highlander,* it should work on fucking Bob!

As Ethan's hand wrapped around the door handle, a thought occurred to him. *This would be a failure.* If he left Bob 'alive,' his one-hundred-percent record would be toast.

The so-called easiest hit he'd had would end his streak.

Would his ego be able to take it?

Could he really walk away?

"For... fuck-sake's... Bob," Ethan squeezed out of his collapsed throat.

As he watched the head tumble closer to the body, he reloaded his pistol and put every bullet into the moving melon. Then he ran and kicked it back across the room, cursing as his mangled foot made contact with the weighty lump.

Ethan jumped up and down on the headless corpse like a kid having a temper tantrum. He tipped the toolbox over and grabbed whatever was at hand.

He started smashing the body with a spanner, breaking through Bob's rib cage with reckless abandon. He took a pair of pliers and began cutting every vein or tendon he could find. He didn't have a clue what half the shit inside Bob was, but he was going to destroy every single bit of it.

Ethan pulled organs from the various holes he created and turned them into shredded chunks with a newly obtained claw hammer. He wrapped his teeth around Bob's intestines and chewed through them as his rage grew, instantly regretting the action as he got a taste of Bob's waste.

He head-butted Bob's kidney until it practically dissolved. Snapped every rib. Put screws through his heart.

Nail gunned his liver. Bent every limb the wrong way, like he was trying to tear them off. Nothing was to be left unharmed.

Ethan stripped Bob's crimson-grey suit from the lower half of his body and took the saw to the dead man's tiny cock and abnormally large balls. He threw them against the living room window and watched as they slowly streaked down the glass, leaving an ugly brown and red smear.

He began hacking at the arms and legs and removing every digit from his hands and feet. Before Ethan knew it, hours had passed. The street outside was dead, and he could now probably get to his car under the cover of darkness, but it didn't matter.

The only thing that needed to be 'dead,' *and had to fucking stay that way,* was Bob.

As the last of the three saws in the toolbox started to lose its sharpness, Ethan grabbed the knife block from the kitchen and carried on his destruction. As he cut through any remaining meaty parts, a new idea struck him, one which signified that insanity had fully taken over.

I know how I'll stop the cunt reforming. I'll fucking eat him!

Where the idea came from was anyone's guess, but the moment it entered Ethan's mind, he couldn't think of anything else.

This was the perfect plan in his mind—the only way to stop Bob.

Plus, maybe it would give him whatever powers Bob had. *That's logical... right?*

Ethan started tossing hacked-off slices of Bob into a frying pan. He placed the remains of Bob's organs in the oven, whacking the temperature up to max. He wasn't a fucking animal, after all. They'd have to be well done.

As the Bob meat cooked, Ethan continued to slice and dice the asshole in a crazed frenzy. No part of the man was left untouched by Ethan's dismantling. There'd be nothing left of him. No evidence Ethan had even killed the man... *However many times it was.*

He'd lost count.

How the fuck do you lose count of how many times you've killed someone?

The answer should always be one!

His whole body had tired long ago, but he wasn't stopping. This was personal. Bob had humiliated him. The fact Bob caused him physical pain in multiple ways was embarrassing enough, but the audacity of not dying was something Ethan couldn't abide.

He'd wipe Bob from the planet.

The oven started to bing, and the smoke alarm blared, breaking Ethan from his reverie. He quickly dashed to the frying pan, burning himself as he put out the small fire flickering from the burnt Bob meat. Even after multiple deaths, the cunt was still causing him pain.

Ethan threw the smoke alarm to the floor and bashed it senseless until the damn thing stopped making a racket.

He took the organs from the oven and plated them up with the fried Bob meat, taking in the sight of the charred remains.

Then he started to devour the bastard.

This will learn him.

Ethan filled his gut with the stubborn cunt, munching down every morsel of the so-called un-killable prick. By the time he'd finished eating Bob, barely anything was left. The little that did remain had been turned to paste and soiled the living room carpet.

"Fuck... You... Bob," Ethan screamed as the final mouthful of the bastard was spat from his mouth.

He gobbled up the escaped meat. *Not taking any chances.*

With that, Ethan collapsed to the floor and slept, filled to the brim on Bob and utterly exhausted from the whole insane ordeal.

A jolt in Ethan's stomach woke him in the early hours. His hands instantly clutched his gut as something began to stir while his tummy rumbled like an overworked washing machine. The sudden wake-up in the strange house left him disoriented, unaware of where he was and why.

... *Bob.*

His mind replayed the previous evening's hit as Ethan stumbled to his feet, cranking his rigid neck after the awkward sleep. His whole body ached. His face felt on fire as he tenderly touched the cheek the skin had hung from. It felt raw and tender, with no sign of the loose peeled skin. A quick glance at the floor would have revealed it, but he dared not look.

Ethan searched for the toilet as bile began to rise in his ruined throat. Something was building in his ass too. Ethan was ready to blow both ends.

The irrational part of his brain, which took over after witnessing the rolling decapitated head, wanted to resist the urge to purge—wanted him to put a cork in his asshole. *Not let Bob escape.* But that was stupid.

He'd eaten a human being. That's what this was.

His body was rebelling and with just cause. Ethan had no doubt that eating Bob was probably worse than snacking on a cheap kebab from some filthy all-night takeaway.

He spotted the bathroom at the top of the landing and began tackling the stairs while his body revolted. He felt feverish. He was sweating from every pour. His muscles ached, bones creaked, blood...*boiled? That couldn't be right.*

Ethan's stomach began to expand. It reminded him of the time he ate too much Indian food, celebrating a job well done after killing a foreign dignitary. He couldn't eat for a day after he was so bloated. 'Never again,' he'd told himself, and stuck with the promise until he filled himself on Bob last night.

But that time, he was just too full—had eaten too much. This was something else. Now, his stomach really was... *expanding?*

Ethan looked down in horror at the movement inside his gut. It wasn't right. He needed to get whatever was inside of him out right away.

He couldn't wait for the toilet.

Ethan yanked his trousers down with every intention of shitting out the spoiled meat there and then. It felt ready to erupt like he'd spray the whole staircase with diarrheic Bob. But nothing would come out.

He stuffed his fingers down his broken throat, trying to puke him up from the other end, but again, nothing would come. He was on the verge of bursting from both holes, yet not a drop.

Tears formed in his eyes as an unimaginable pain took hold. *This isn't right.* Something was horribly wrong. This wasn't a bad case of food poisoning or some viral thing he'd picked up. His whole body felt awkwardly tense while his stomach continued to slowly expand.

He begged his ass to shit—was desperate for the relief that would accompany a satisfying dump. But he still couldn't make it happen.

Then his mind moved away from his throbbing asshole as a hand burst through his chest.

Ethan couldn't quite take in what was happening. At first, he laughed; it was so unbelievable laughter felt like the only reaction. Then he started slapping his raw cheek, trying to wake himself from the visceral nightmare because this *really* couldn't be happening.

But Ethan was already awake and knew a hand really had punched a hole through him, from the inside, no less. It was followed up a second later as his guts spilt to the floor. He recognised some of the spillage as the body parts leaked from him, reminding him of his recent rummage through Bob.

A foot exploded from his own, sending him tumbling down the stairs with his head barrelling over his bare ass. Still, the shit wouldn't come.

As Ethan lay dazed on the floor, he felt his mouth opening unnaturally wide. Something was crawling from his throat and prying his jaw open. One of his eyes popped from the socket and dangled beside his cheek. As the optic nerve swung, Ethan caught sight of his mouth, and Bob's head was impossibly emerging from it.

What the fuck, Bob? Ethan thought one last time before his body exploded into showery lumps of gore, and the rest of Bob burst out of him.

Bob sat naked on the sofa in the living room after his rebirth. He stared at the bloody stain on the carpet when his phone rang.

"How the fuck are you still alive," a voice questioned from the other end, clearly surprised Bob had answered.

"I told you. I can't be killed."

And He was Forsaken

by Stuart Bray

It was the year of our lord, 1876. I was but a boy, soon to be a man. My father pulled the strap from the barn wall, his eyes red in a drunken rage. "Come on over, boy! Let me see under those trousers. Hurry up, boy, I don't have all night!"

I reluctantly pulled down the back of the trousers that my mother had sewn me last fall.

"Lean on over that rail. Time to get what's due."

I closed my eyes, leaning over the wooden rail next to where we once kept the pigs that were now long dead from sickness. The warm night air brushed against my bare buttocks. The first lash came without warning, sounding like a branch snapping from the top of a giant oak.

"I won't stop, boy. Not until I see blood." My father stumbled; I knew because I could hear the loose straw crushing under his filthy feet.

Another crack with the leather strap, this time the pain much worse than before. I didn't want to cry. A man should not cry no matter what horrors he is faced with. After three more loud snaps, I passed out from the pain.

"Did you have to beat him so hard? He's but a boy, Agustus." My mother patted my face with a wet cloth as the small room slowly came into focus.

"He wants to be a man in my home, he needs to be beaten like one." I could see my father sitting next to the fireplace, the once roaring fire now just glowing embers floating like fireflies up the chimney. "You will do well to keep your lips closed. No good will come if you are shown in town with a beaten face of your own." My father took another swig from his cup. "Fix him up, get him back on his feet. I'll need him to chop the wood tomorrow. The boy is no use if he cannot contribute the strength of his youth."

The sun burned my face. I had finished my many hours of chopping wood and was on to my next task.

"Get those creek rocks from the forest, boy." My father pointed towards the opening in the trees near our cottage.

I hesitated, dropping the axe to the ground at my feet. "But, father, the forest is—"

My father growled, pulling himself up from the log where he sat. "If I have to tell you again that there is no goddamned witch in those woods, I'll break you where you stand!"

I swallowed, my throat dry from thirst. I had heard stories my entire life—stories about the old woman who lived in the woods, a woman covered in the fur of animals, a wicked old witch who snatched children from their beds as they slept.

"Take the cart and get that damn creek rock. I want it placed neatly behind the cottage, you hear?" My father used the pile of chopped wood behind him to control balance. I saw my mother through the window, her face stricken with unbearable sadness.

"Yes, father." I lowered my head, fetching the cart next to the old outhouse. The trees up ahead were tall and barren. I had never once seen a leaf grow from their long, armlike limbs. I should have prayed before this task. I should have asked God to watch over me, to guide me safely through this dreadful, devil-ridden place.

The cart creaked loudly as I pushed it down the overgrown path. The tall trees blackened the sun more and more the deeper I traveled. I whistled aloud, a hymn I had heard countless times in church. Anything was better than the unbearable silence that followed me so closely. I wondered why these woods were so different from the rest. Why did all of the trees look like giant monsters reaching out to grab you up by the collar of your shirt?

"You live on the witch's land! You and your family share the woods with the devil!" I remembered an old man screaming at me on the road as he passed by on his wagon, his eyes white, his teeth as black as the deepest pit.

I asked my mother when I arrived home what the old man was talking about. She just stared at me as she hung up my father's sleeping gown on the clothesline out back. "Don't you be speaking of such things in front of your father. You know he forbids such talk under his roof."

I came upon the creek. The bed ran softly with fresh, clear water. But even the sound of the water was muffled by the thick, dreadful silence that the woods seemed to horde an abundance of.

I lifted the first rock. The water made it difficult to grip, and I almost dropped it on my toe. After filling the cart with more rocks than I could ever transport with ease, I was stopped by the sounds of a woman singing in the distance.

I glanced around for a moment, wondering if it was my mother. I knew she enjoyed singing while washing clothes. Was it *her* that I was listening to through the trees? "Mother? I called out. I waited a moment for a response, but there was none. The singing continued, sounding even closer this time. "Hello?" I called.

The singing stopped once more but then sounded closer once starting back up again. The voice and its song were both unfamiliar to me. What was this song? It was one I had never heard in church. I listened closer, listening to the words.

"The children's cries, their painful moans, a gleeful tool, for my cheerful tone. Listen now, hear my call, come take my hand, I'll take you all."

The singing stopped, and I was again buried alive by the forest and its defensive silence. "Hello, who's there? This is *my* father's land. You had better leave at once!" The threat of my father scared only *me*, sending a chill down the back of my neck Before I could grab my cart of rocks and run, my feet were yanked out from underneath me, causing my body to smack against the side of the creek bed. For a few moments, I was dazed, the trees around me spinning out of control. "Mother!" I screamed before being dragged further down the creek bed.

I tried my best to kick free from the invisible force that held tightly to my ankles, pulling me further and further away from my cart. Then, in the blink of an eye, I shot upwards, my legs dangling in midair. "Mother! Help me!" I screamed as loud as I could as the invisible force pulled my pants off. "No!" I cried as a sharp pain shot through my body.

Right before I clenched my eyes shut from the pain, I could see an old woman standing below me, her nude body covered in a thick black fur. I was paralyzed by fear, the worst fear I had ever felt in my life.

I opened my eyes once my body dropped to the forest floor below. The woman had vanished. A warm sensation came from my rear. I reached back to feel, and when I brought my hand back, it was covered in blood.

I cried.

I cried as I pulled up my pants. I cried as I walked back to the cart. I cried all the way back home.

"Where were you, boy? It doesn't take all day to fetch creek rock. I bet you were fiddling around like a lazy dog, weren't you?" my father shouted from the doorway of the small cottage.

I dropped to my knees before getting the cart to the spot my father had asked me to place it in. At this point, every breath felt like a fight for survival.

"Get up, boy! You had plenty of time to rest when you were neglecting your duties. Get back to work, or I'll tan your hide!" My father grabbed a plank of wood from the old pile he kept on the side of the house. He smacked the palm of his hand with it, his eyes growing furious.

"Father, something happened in the woods. I can't explain it, but it felt like the devil took hold of me!" I used the handles of the cart to pull myself back to my feet. My legs shook uncontrollably.

"Nonsense! You are a liar, boy! There are no devils here. This is the lord's land, blessed by the church and prayed upon every single day!" My father approached me, the wooden plank hanging in his right hand. "I'll beat that devil talk right out of you, boy! I will not have it in my house!"

My mother ran to my father's side, a look of panic and worry on her tired old face. "Let the boy be, please. He has worked hard for the lord today. Please, let him rest."

Without hesitation, my father used the back of his left hand to strike my mother in the side of the face. "Keep your mouth shut. Don't you ever tell me how to run the home that I alone built from nothing. Your sympathy for this useless excuse of a boy has been a thorn in my side as of late. I will tolerate it no longer."

I truly have no idea how I did it or where I mustered the strength, but I charged my father, taking him to the ground.

"How dare you? How dare you raise your hand to—"

Before my father could get back to his feet, I used the wooden plank he had dropped to bash him in the back of the head. I did this until my father went silent—until his body moved no more.

"What have you done?" my mother cried out, crawling to my father's side.

"He was an evil man, mother. He deserved it. You know he deserved it!" I pleaded, clasping my hands tightly in prayer. "Lord, forgive me, for I know not what I have done!"

My mother continued sobbing so loudly that the birds flew from the nearby trees.

A sharp and familiar pain shot up my backside, causing me to fall to my side. "Mother!" I cried out as something pushed its way out of my body. "It hurts!" I screamed.

My mother rushed to my side. "It's a punishment. I just know it!" She took my head in her hands, resting it on her knees.

"Please, make it stop!" I begged, the pain growing worse.

"The devils have come. They've come to take us for our sins!"

I looked up to where my mother was now pointing her finger. A group of naked old women huddled together, approaching us slowly.

"Who are you? What are you doing on our land?" my mother asked, quickly getting to her feet. "If you have come for my son, you can take him. Please, just leave me be!"

The nude old women whispered to each other as they got closer and closer.

"Take him and leave this place! Leave this place now!" my mother screamed over and over again, backing towards the cottage.

In my pain-induced daze, I could see there were five of the nude women, each of them old and decrepit, their hair as white as winter snow.

"It dwells within him. It dwells within him. It dwells within him."

The old women were close enough now that I could smell their horrendous odor. Their fingernails were long and dirty. Their sagging skin flapped as they walked.

"Stay away from me, please. I have done nothing to offend you!" I hoped my mother would help me. I hoped she would scare the women off with threats of fire and brimstone, but she just stood there, watching as these old witches huddled around me.

"Dear Lord, I pray to thee in this hour of need. I pray that you forgive me for my sins and lead me into your kingdom of heaven." I closed my eyes, hoping it would shield me from the hands tugging at my clothes. My eyes opened at the screams of my mother. More of the old woman had appeared, pulling at my mother's arms.

"Leave me be, leave me be, you harlots of Satan!" My mother's arms were yanked from the sockets, the flesh ripped with ease. Blood sprayed in every direction.

"This land belongs not to your god but to the beast. Your trespass is a blessing to Him, an offering to our Father."

My mother dropped to her knees before having her head yanked from her shoulders. What was left of her body crumbled to the ground.

I kicked and scratched at the witches, freeing myself from their grasp. "I'll leave this land! I'll leave this place and never return! I swear to it!" I screamed, not looking over my shoulder as I ran as fast as possible. The sound of the witches' cackles echoed behind me as I reached the dirt road beyond the fence.

"Thank you, Lord, thank you!" I cried, dropping to my knees to catch my breath.

Feeling wicked eyes upon me, I turned to see the old women lined up along the fence, their bodies covered in the blood of my mother. "I've fled from your land. What else do you ask of me, you wicked spawns of hell?"

I tried to get back to my feet to run even further than I had already, but I couldn't budge. That pain returned; this time, it was in the pit of my stomach. "What did you do to me in the forest? what did you put inside of me?" I cried, touching my belly from under my shirt. "Lord, help me,"

I whispered, feeling something move under my pale white flesh.

"It dwells within. It dwells within. It dwells within." The old witches chanted loudly, holding hands with one another, forming a chain as long and as far as the eye could see.

"The devil is inside of me. I am but a vessel, nothing more." A voice whispered in my ear.

I turned, but there was no one there. I wanted to scream at the old witches. I wanted to curse them, damn them to the hell from which they came, but they were *there* no more.

I knew I had seen the last of the old women, but the gift they left behind grew inside me. I never returned to my father's land, nor did I ever think back on the horrors of that day.

I arrived at the train station with a suitcase in tow. Running my fingers through my thick mustache, I pulled my ticket from my jacket pocket.

"Howdy there, Mister. Fine day we're having!" The conductor approached me, his hand reaching for my ticket.

"Sure is," I responded, tipping my hat.

"Heck of a name you got there, Mister. What does the H.H stand for?" the conductor asked, handing me back the ticket he had just punched.

I looked down at the small piece of paper before sticking it back in my pocket. "Henry Howard. the name's Henry Howard Holmes." I sat back in my seat, stroking my mustache once more.

"Trian to Chicago, all aboard!" the conductor shouted.

Feed the Earth
by Christy Aldridge

Carl was sick and tired of digging. At seventy-two years old, such work should have been left to the children and grandchildren. That was the goal when you decided to own a farm. It was property to hand down to the young ones. However, Betsey was barren. In the fifty-three years they had been married, she never even had a pregnancy scare.

The lack of children didn't bother Carl until it came to manual labor. In the early years, he and Betsey could handle it all on their own. Back then, the farm belonged to her daddy. But it was theirs now. Had been for the last forty years or so. They never had trouble handling the cattle they raised or the various farm animals they considered pets.

When they began to advance in years, Betsey suggested hiring a couple of young boys to help out. It worked out for a while. Two young boys, needing a little extra cash, would come and help them out. But they eventually moved on to higher-paying jobs.

The boys were a difficult bunch to pick from. After the first two, Carl found himself dealing with young men who were either lazy or thieves. After one boy stole his tractor, despite how his dad insisted he didn't, Betsey stopped wanting strangers to come to the farm. After all, the tractor had belonged to her daddy.

After that, they sold most of the herd of cows, sticking to the pets they could take care of with no problem. They kept two cows. Both were milking cows and Betsey's favorite pets. She never complained about milking either one, even on days when Carl could tell her arthritis was acting up.

She loved the cows. Bertha and Gerta were her babies.

Then Bertha decided to die.

Carl understood why. The cow was old. She had lived out her purpose. Betsey was heartbroken all the same. Carl wanted to get rid of her body as quickly as he could to keep from upsetting Betsey even more, but when he hooked Bertha to the truck to move her to his burn pit, Betsey threw a fit.

"You're not burning my baby," Carl said now, mocking her voice in an awful interpretation. He was still mad about it. He and Betsey didn't fight much anymore. Neither had the time or energy. Truthfully, there wasn't a whole lot worth fighting about at their age. But being told he needed to bury the cow was enough to anger him—especially when she couldn't help because her back was giving her trouble.

It didn't matter if his back was troubling him. Her only solution to that was to ask one of the neighbors to dig the hole, but Carl wouldn't do that. He didn't like the neighbors, and although he had yet to tell her, the truck was acting up again. It was likely only a loose spark plug or wire, but he refused to ask the neighbors to do a job he didn't want to do himself.

So, it boiled down to him. *He* had to dig the hole—and not just any hole. Bertha was a large cow, as cows were apt to be, and he had to dig a hole wide enough to hold her and deep enough to keep her stench from bothering them for the next few weeks while she decayed underground.

He had waited until around four to start because the sun would be lower in the sky, and it would be cooler. He dug all afternoon and evening, and the hole still needed to be deeper before he could shove the cow inside. Then he'd still have to bury it. It would be close to his bedtime by the time he got inside.

His shovel struck something hard. Carl looked down but only saw the dirt. He shoved his shovel at the ground and, once again, struck something hard. When he forced some of the dirt away, he realized it was a rock.

"Great. Just great!" he grumbled.

He reached out of the hole and felt around the grass for the pickaxe. When his hand landed on it, he pulled it into the hole and began hacking away at the hard earth.

Carl didn't expect the area he was hitting to collapse. The rock was thinner than he'd expected. As the earth caved in, he could see the empty ground beneath.

In all the years he had been alive, he'd never seen the earth do that. Digging deep and hitting water—yes. Digging up random objects—yes. Digging through rock and finding an empty layer of earth—no.

He got to his knees and peered into the hole. It was wet inside. He heard the small trickle of water and felt coolness coming up from the ground.

Groundwater? It was the only thing he could think of. He'd never seen it, but he had heard there were pockets of water deep in the earth. But less than five feet down? Was that even possible? And to have one in his backyard was a strange occurrence, but it seemed like the only logical answer.

Then something moved.

Carl jumped back, hitting the edge of the hole and knocking dirt onto his head. He growled and cursed as he shook it out of his hair.

Then he stopped. The thing that moved before moved closer to the opening. Carl could see it clearly from where he sat but couldn't believe what he was staring at.

The thing inside the hole looked like a blob of shiny gelatin with teeth. Rows of teeth were everywhere, indicating that it didn't have one mouth but many. All teeth were sharp and curved, with one set formed around a set of long, snake-like tongues. Eyes were everywhere—large, round balls protruding from its body like globes filled with blue and purple water. The liquid in the eyes swished as it pulled itself with its tentacles. Some of the tentacles had spikes poking through the skin, giving it more grip when it pulled its flat, pink body along the rock.

Carl immediately thought it looked like a flat, mutated octopus. The way it moved its body reminded him of how an octopus would pull itself out of its tank or walk across the seafloor, but it was also clear that this was no ordinary octopus. It was likely not any relation at all.

When the creature got to the opening, it shuddered back and shrieked. Carl jumped at the sound and covered his ears. A small gust of smoke rose from the hole as the creature pulled itself into the darkness.

"Too sensitive for the sun?" Carl asked it. Not that he expected it to answer. He mostly said it to convince himself.

But the sun was going down. Carl could see it casting a shadow over the opening. The creature was moving closer to the opening again. It was shy, Carl thought—shy and afraid. Perhaps the thing had never seen a human before. He could almost guarantee that a human had never seen whatever it was. Something like this would have been plastered across TV screens if discovered.

"And maybe I'm gonna be rich for discovering a new creature," he said, grinning as he watched the blob with growing interest. It was ugly. The sight of it was almost too unreal to believe. If he hadn't been staring at it with his own eyes, he might have guessed it was one of those special effects from movies or TV shows.

One of its arms wrapped around Carl's leg in the blink of an eye. It jerked Carl from his position and pulled half of his leg into the hole with it.

"Ow!" Carl grunted, landing on his butt. He could feel the sliminess of its tentacles against his skin. Sharp little barbs slid over his jeans and then touched his bare skin, and he realized it was chewing on his jeans. Ripping the denim off at the knee, his bare leg was exposed under the ground.

He tried to pull his leg out, but it wasn't moving. It barely budged as he used all his strength to pull at it. The tentacles held a firm grasp on his exposed skin, and they weren't letting it go.

Then, a new sensation... A slimy feeling slid up his leg, but he could move. He scooted back, pulling his leg out of the hole.

But the creature hadn't let him go. His foot was inside one of its mouths. The mouth was stretched to a terrifying size, wrapped entirely around his ankle and moving up. It used its teeth to pull forward against his skin. The creature was trying to devour him.

"Get off of me! Get off of me!" Carl screamed, thrashing his legs about. He knew he had kicked the creature in the face, wherever its face was. The dozens of eyes throughout its slimy body made it hard to know where its face was.

A few of its eyes had crumpled. They were bleeding a blueish-purple goo beneath, but it did nothing to stop the creature from slowly chewing its way up his leg. Most of the blood on the creature's face had come from Carl's leg as his foot disappeared further into its mouth inch by devastating inch. Carl clawed at the ground but found nothing to hold to.

Worse yet, he could see his leg through the creature's translucent flesh. As it consumed more of his leg, its gelatinous body stretched and became clear. He could see his leg inside it like he was looking into water.

It's going to eat my leg, Carl thought.

Carl felt the teeth pulling him. He could feel them retracting like a snake's teeth when swallowing prey. Perhaps the creature was part snake, Carl thought in his terrified state of mind. Like a snake, it would unhinge its jaws and swallow him before returning to the darkness to sleep.

Carl felt the teeth stop pulling. He screamed as they bit down. Rows of teeth dug deeply into his skin before the creature sprung back like a rubber band and completely skinned his leg and foot. Carl was too shocked to breathe as he stared at the clean bone. Like removing a shirt sleeve, all skin and muscle had been stripped from the bone. Only traces of blood remained.

The creature was gnawing on his leg, chewing through meat and muscle before Carl could catch his breath. As he began to breathe with labored gasps, a sharp pain entered his chest. *A heart attack?* He could feel it, but he wasn't sure if the sudden pain was any worse than having his leg eaten like a chicken leg—picked clean and chewed before his very eyes.

But the creature wasn't done. One tentacle reached out and grabbed the leg bone, pulled it with enough force to rip it from the joint, and shoved it straight into another mouth. Carl's mind fought to comprehend everything around him.

His mouth, however, only knew to scream.

Carl's screams turned to high-pitched squeals. He pulled himself away from the opening but couldn't do much else. His leg was *gone.* The creature was pulling its body out of the hole and was considerably larger. Still, it was very gelatin-like, not so much bending as it was molding to each new surface it reached. Its eyes were swishing everywhere, the ones that weren't crushed.

Carl knew it was looking at him. He could barely focus straight, seeing even more eyes the longer he stared at it. Whether it was because of the sharp chest pain spreading through his body or the blood loss from his leg, he wasn't sure.

It flicked its tongues. Carl once heard that snakes often flicked their tongues in the air to taste it to tell what types of prey were around them. When the creature threw out one of its tooth-covered tentacles and attached it to his throat, Carl realized he was the closest prey.

His leg had only been an appetizer.

As the creature stretched over his torso, it removed the tentacle from Carl's neck and replaced it with another smaller mouth. This mouth chewed on his throat, silencing any more screams as it tore into his flesh and had its meal.

Carl could see the rest of the creature's body sprouting off. Instead of one human-sized blob, there were multiple gelatinous blobs, each with its own teeth and eyes. They sprouted legs from their bodies like a hydra growing heads.

But the one on his throat remained, chewing and sucking the blood that Carl was beginning to choke on. Another one was at his hand, sliding the skin and muscle from his fingers like it was sucking meat from a crawfish.

Carl wasn't aware of how long the creature had chewed on his jugular, but he was still conscious enough to see some of the others moving away from him. Carl choked on his blood as the many arms lifted them above the dirt and out of the hole. Until the sun rose again, he knew this creature would wreak havoc. It would probably eat the rest of the animals the same way it had eaten his leg.

Then, when Betsey began to worry, as she was apt to do, it would attack her. His poor Betsey. She'd be dead—just like Bertha.

Just like him.

Full Nasty
Dan Shrader

"Alright, well, you wanted it! And now you got it, Fuck-Fans! We just got a fresh one for you. Another Full Nasty! Quick disclaimer: if you're a squeamish little bitch, then this is not for you!" with an evil chuckle, the announcer stressed the last sentence once again. "I mean, this shit ain't for everybody."

The camera slowly zoomed out, revealing a distressing scene. A woman was bound to a chair, her body unable to move. A dirty rag was shoved in her mouth to silence any pleas for help. Blood stains all over her body were a harsh contrast against her pale complexion.

A hand covered in blood emerged from the frame, gently caressing her hair. "Don't be scared, little momma. You're about to experience the best fuck of your life!"

The room around this frightened girl was disgusting and littered with broken furniture, homemade torture instruments, and sex devices. Off in the lay a fresh, mutilated corpse of another girl. Blood still poured from her cracked skull.

This was a playground for the sick and depraved.

A raw image of hell on earth.

"You all ready to get in this hell-wagon? You ready for a motherfuckin' ride?" The man screamed, forcefully slamming his face into the camera lens and leaving a smudge. He took a step back and let the camera focus. Then. He casually put on a trucker hat with the bold words "LOT LIZZARD" across the top. "This is Satanic Bill, along with my tribe of termites—the Fuck Brothers! Sit back Fuck-Fans, 'cause we got us a Full Nasty comin' at ya now."

Bill's dark and menacing on-camera demeanor was terrifying. He exuded inbred mannerisms and behavior enough to send chills down anyone's spine. His decaying teeth and patchy, unkempt facial hair added to his unsettling appearance. An unsettling display of Nazi symbols and clippings from adult magazines decorated the walls around him.

"Oh, yeah... this is take, or reel number..." he paused for a moment. "Klegg? Klegg, you dirty bitch hog! Come here!"

"What, Bill?" Klegg inquired as he came into view. Other than the child's Halloween mask he wore, he was completely naked. He had the physique of a sturdy country boy with a bit of extra weight. A dragon tattoo stretched across his upper arm, wrapping from bicep to forearm. But the most striking feature about Klegg was his extraordinarily large and erect cock stretching out in front of him.

Klegg's penis extended so forcefully that it came dangerously close to poking Bill's side when he rushed into frame.

"Hey, watch out with that thing, you damn baboon!" Bill chuckled, brushing it off as if it were nothing. He shifted his attention back to the camera. "So, what episode number are we on?"

"Hell, I don't know boss..."

"And why is that?" Bill aggressively asked.

"Because..." Klegg faltered, struggling to find a coherent answer. He appeared almost nervous, stumbling over his words as he pondered the question.

"Because why?" Bill asked, turning to Klegg to give him a small signal—something they had shared earlier.

A tense silence filled the air as the two locked eyes. Suddenly, they shifted their gaze toward the camera and let out a simultaneous scream:

"BECAUSE-WE-CAME-HERE-TO-FUCK!!"

This was one of hundreds of videos for these backwoods degenerates. Since the beginning, their films kept getting smuttier and nastier, eventually blossoming into FULL NASTY. Klegg and his brothers had been acquainted with Satanic Bill for the last ten years. Bill was like a father figure, a brother, hell, even a cousin, all wrapped up in one. Some would say he was their own personal fucked up Jesus.

The townsfolk referred to the boys as the "Fuck Brothers" because—well—it sounded that way. It was spelled P-H-U-C-K, and with a last name like that, they were destined to endure ridicule day in and out.

Some would argue that a person's upbringing didn't influence their future, but these boys never had a fighting chance. The Fuck Brothers didn't have a particularly easy upbringing in the county. But, just like any mistreated pups, they had the ever-loving shit beat out of them constantly and grew up more twisted than ever.

Being raised by a single mother who worked as a stripper and living in a run-down trailer park didn't help matters much. In the trailer park, their family were the rich ones and highly respected. Their momma screwed half the police force and any other *John* who could pay.

Then, one day, a large carnival arrived in town, and their momma instantly fell in love with the tall, skinny man by the Ferris wheel. Satanic Bill was that tall drink of water. He came to like living in the county so much that he decided to quit his job and stay with them. They moved out of the trailer park and got a beaten-down farmhouse in the middle of a desolate stretch of land. The initial aim was to get away from the nosey neighbors.

But it would soon turn into a house of misery, as one morning, Momma was found dead, face down in a bowl of Cheerios. The Fuck Brothers were never the same after that, and Satanic Bill made sure of it.

Bill pressed the cold silver button on the device, starting the conveyor on the machine. Klegg watched intently as the lifeless body descended gradually from upstairs to the basement, landing with a hollow thud on the stained metal table.

The house was equipped with hatches in every room, providing a convenient pulley system to easily transport bodies up and down. Bill had come up with the idea years ago when he felt overworked by manually carrying the deceased up and down the stairs. Of course, they were handling the bodies in the same way they do now.

The final straw that convinced them to add the pulley system came one night when Klegg, in a drunken state, attempted to carry two bodies up the stairs. The withered steps couldn't bear the weight and split while he was mid-step. Klegg tumbled headfirst from the top. The impact resulted in a head injury, significantly affecting his cognitive abilities. Bill already knew Klegg wasn't the sharpest tool in the shed, but the fall impaired his skills even more.

"She sure is purdy, Bill."

"Don't you mean 'was'?" Bill responded, his laughter filled with wickedness. Klegg joined in, as he always did.

Her lifeless body lay sprawled before them, completely exposed. Her face, devoid of color, appeared ghostly in the dim light while her eyes remained wide open, frozen in a haunting state of disbelief. For them, this moment, which most would find extremely unsettling, was a precious ritual they enjoyed together.

"I believe we broke this one, my friend," Bill said, dabbing her face with his weathered fingertips. "Yes, indeed, we tamed the beast in her, without a doubt." Bill firmly smacked her ass before swiftly redirecting his attention to the tool table and pointing. The seamless motion was executed with a touch of theatrical flair. "Gimme the Phillips, my boy!" Bill declared in a deep baritone.

Bill's theatrics made Klegg jump excitedly as he rushed toward the tool table.

"Comin' right up!"

Lighting a cigarette and taking a large puff, Bill took a moment and leaned down face to face with the corpse. "Was it as good for you as it was for us, little momma?" The air reeked of fatty flesh, feces, and the unmistakable stench of death.

For Bill, the act of killing was his ultimate thrill. It was a rush unlike anything else in this entire shitty world. The exhilarating mix of whiskey and cocaine on a gangbang with the boys was fun. "Black Dog" by Led Zeppelin only added to the adrenaline coursing through his veins at such an event. But, for Bill, everything paled in comparison to the euphoria of murder and torture.

Bill casually threw the remaining chicken bones onto the table, adding them to the enormous pile. He enjoyed his wings, messy and dripping with sauce, and washing them down with some cheap, ice-cold beer. The cheaper and stronger, the better. His philosophy applied to more than just food and drink. It extended to his preferences for pussy. The dirtier, the better.

"I feel the market is getting saturated with the same shit," Bill barked, clearly frustrated and still hungry for more wings. He dug his hands into the box. "I need you little pig fuckers to think of something good and quick. The old man down at the Emporium ain't gonna buy this shit no more if we can't think of something new."

"Something new? We coined the word Full Nasty, Bill. That's us," Chunk blurted out, hastily reaching for a wing, only to have his hand smacked away. He should have known better. That was Bill's portion of the wing box.

"Yeah, we got a good thing goin'. Why do we need something new?" Klegg asked. He happily leaned over and grabbed a wing from Bill's box, and Bill didn't mind. Of the three, Klegg was Bill's favorite, and the others knew it. "Come on, Bill. What's there to make new about it all? You know I'm good as long as I get a nut."

Bill shook his head and glanced at the others seated around the table. "Well, it looks like we've got a group of NASA-fucking-rocket-boys here," he exclaimed with a hint of sarcasm. "You guys just don't grasp the market. But fear not, Satanic Bill is here to enlighten your hearts and minds."

He pointed at the wall where a black phone hung beside the regular house line. Its hand-painted exterior showed signs of shoddy craftsmanship. "Unless that phone rings with a market request, we're left to our own devices to create something...something fucking new! And let's face it. We haven't been doing that for a while now!"

"I mean, I'll film anything," Chunk exclaimed. "Buster here went and had his way with a damn barn goat last week. The sight of it nearly made me lose my breakfast. It was disgusting, Bill—nasty! But I did it for the sake of our films."

Bill closed his eyes. He downed the last of his stale, bitter, cheap beer and swiftly altered his approach. Opening his eyes and flashing a smile at the boys, he began, "I have never doubted your complete dedication to the projects. You guys are true artists. Klegg, my friend, you are the star. And Chunk and Buster...well, you two are simply...irreplaceable."

As if he had been saved by the bell, the black phone started chirping and ringing endlessly. Excitement invaded the air around them, taking over everyone's somber moods. Chunk jumped up from his seat and accidentally knocked over his chair.

"Well, praise the dark lord!" Bill exclaimed, hurling his beer can with precision, striking Buster in the mouth.

Chunk or Buster always seemed to catch something whenever the opportunity arose. Bill found joy in the little things that made life amusing.

Chunk pressed the receiver to his ear, breathing heavily. He listened intently as the dial tone beeped and buzzed, indicating the connection was being made. "It's a call from one of the bosses," he said, glancing at the others.

Bill dropped his wing and smacked his hands together. "I'm tellin' ya they want something big this time."

"Hold on," Chunk said, holding out his hand. "It's connecting."

"Yep, yep, yep!" Klegg exclaimed, his voice brimming with enthusiasm as he eagerly reached for another wing. "It's definitely important," he mumbled, relishing every mouth-watering bite.

The unique phone line was reserved for the highest bidders of the black market—those who sought the forbidden, from the grotesque world of torture porn to the carnal cravings of a cannibal's grocery list. It was a portal for their darkest desires, a gateway to consume something or someone in ways unimaginable. When the phone rang, Bill knew it was a cash cow on the other line.

"Incoming...From...Black...Priest...6...6...6..." a robot voice transmitted, "Message...For... Satanic...Bill...Password...Please."

"Bill, this is only for you. It's gotta be huge!" Chunk exclaimed with excitement. "It's one of those password-protected ones too!" He couldn't contain his enthusiasm as he practically leaped out of his shoes, rushing to hand the phone to Bill from across the room.

Wiping his greasy fingers on his t-shirt, Bill picked up the receiver and placed it against his ear. "This is the devil, ready to carry out the devil's work."

"Access...Granted..." the robot replied, as a loud ring suddenly filled the air.

Persephone Jones always felt the eyes of everyone burning holes in her back when she went to the grocery store. The townspeople couldn't help it. She was different and weird to them.

She was a tall, long-legged brunette with dazzling green eyes that could put any man in a trance. The green eyes were something of a family thing. Everyone she knew in her community had them, too. Persephone was raised to believe she was unique from the rest of the world.

"You always fear what you cannot understand," her benevolent patriarch would tell them as children. Perse-

phone belonged to a commune, or as the locals loved to say out loud, "a cult."

The commune was located on the outskirts of Buzzard's Bay, the town where she shopped.

Faora was formed during the Vietnam War by several college elite, hippies, and activists. It was a sustainable colony of peace-loving people who wanted nothing to do with the outside world. Over the last decade, things had changed. They mingled more with the locals and left their secluded timber lodges to interact with others. Persephone initially thought it was weird, but she'd grown accustomed to it.

Taking her items to the cashier, Persephone caught a glimpse of a beaten and battered white van sitting in the parking lot. It had been parked by the doorway for a long time. The men in the van stared at her. But they didn't stare like the others. Their gazes seemed predatory.

In the hammered van, Bill reclined in the driver's seat, a cherry-flavored sucker held between his lips, its sugary taste filling his mouth. His sunglasses rested on the bridge of his nose as he gazed through the smudged glass windows of the supermarket. Seated beside him, Klegg anxiously scanned the sprawling parking lot, his eyes darting from one car to another. In the back, Buster and Chunk fidgeted restlessly, their energy barely contained in the confined space.

"She sure is purdy, Bill."

"That she is, Klegg. That one is a rare beauty indeed."

"What's so special about her?"

"She's pure. She's the forbidden fruit, boys," Bill explained. "Comes from a cult up the road. There are plenty like her, too. Never had a request like this before."

The blindfold and gag didn't make Persephone uncomfortable.

It was the way her captors treated her body that did. The smelly, greasy bastards—putting their hands all over her breasts the way they did. She was scared but knew she had to keep calm. Their words and touch made her feel inferior.

When she'd seen the van door open, a sickening feeling had washed over her. Her hands were full of groceries, and everything seemed to blur together in a whirlwind of images and emotions.

At that moment, trapped in the van with no help, she realized she was in serious trouble. She felt hands groping her and heard their terrible music—the devilish tunes they sang as they took her on this unwanted road trip. She tried to retreat into her mind, but each time, she was interrupted by two of them kissing her, groping, and whispering perverted nothings into her ears.

Persephone wanted to vomit.

She tried to drown them out with a simple hymn her mother had taught her. But this only made Persephone angrier and more frustrated. So, she did her best to keep calm and not fight back. Unless that's what they wanted, she needed to stay alive.

Their words were like toxic venom in her ears. As each syllable spewed forth from their rotten mouths, she could taste their breath.

Persephone had never heard such crude and offensive language before, especially from men. It disgusted her how they vividly described the sexual acts they intended to perform on her. Many of the terms were unfamiliar, as she was raised in a tradition of abstinence until marriage—a practice followed by most in her community. This was known as the Faora way.

As they entered the house, a putrid and repulsive stench invaded her nostrils, assaulting her senses. The air reeked of urine, decaying flesh, and the musk of dirty dishes. The foul odor lingered in an unsettling way, causing her stomach to churn with a wave of nausea.

They carried her along. Persephone didn't fight as they dragged her. She continued to remind herself to fight the smell and the fear—to remain calm and focus on where she came from and who she was.

At last, she found herself on a sofa saturated with all the house's terrible odors, its broken springs engulfing her. As her weight sunk into the mangy cushion, the stench invaded her nostrils with deplorable ease.

First, the gag was taken off, and then the blindfold.

She studied each of the four men, trying to read their expressions and gauge their true intentions. Each possessed a unique form of ugliness that was repulsive to behold. Persephone gave them each a look that could kill.

Bill smirked at her anger. "This one's a fighter, boys," he warned, moving forward and eyeing her up and down. "There is something special about you girls from that commune up there."

"What's so special about 'em," Klegg asked with a smile.

"He already said, stupid. The buyer said they were special. He's paying for this show, so if he says they're special, they're special," Chunk snapped, seeming surprised by Klegg's stupidity.

"No. It's something more than that. There is something extraordinary about the women in this...cult," Bill corrected Chunk.

"We are not a cult. Just because your people do not understand our ways doesn't mean you have to label us so," She protested, gritting her teeth.

Bill rushed over and slapped his finger on her lip. "It's a cult. Do you know why? Because I fuckin' said so, bitch! You understand? Now, shut the fuck up and only speak when I tell you to. Got it?"

She nodded slowly.

"You mean to tell me you all hiding in that little community aren't all related? It's like you all have some backwards ass genes or something. Never seen no inbreeders have such beautiful offspring."

"Yeah! Your daddy and mommy are related!" Chunk poked fun.

Bill shot Chunk a glare, causing him to shrink away. "Your mom and dad were first cousins, shit for brains! How can you make fun of her?"

Chunk cast his gaze to the floor.

"You're in for a real treat," Bill declared, thrusting his crotch in Persephone's direction. "You're about to experience what we like to call The Full Nasty!"

Bill snapped his fingers in Chunk's face and said, "Now, can I trust you two idiots to stay here with her while we go to the Emporium to drop off the latest stag films?"

Buster's head was bobbing like crazy, and his smile was huge. Chunk's eyes met his, a questioning gaze filled with curiosity. "Why you gotta say it like that?"

"Why? Why do I have to say it like that? Because of you, dildo! The last time you messed up..." Bill glanced at Klegg before flicking his zippo to light his cigarette. "Almost lost the merchandise!"

"I promise. I promise. This time will be different," Chunk exclaimed. "We've got this. She's tied up and locked in the room."

"The trap door is bolted, right?" Bill asked.

"Yeah, Bill. I'll double-check—"

"No. Don't go in there," Bill said, exhaling a cloud of smoke before pointing at the television. "You two, just watch cartoons and relax."

"Jesus. All right, Bill," Chunk conceded without further argument. He was determined to show their capability to monitor the house. "Go do it. We got this."

"Remember, this one is crucial," Bill explained to all three of them, waving the cigarette in their faces. "The customer on the phone wants her completely ruined. A Full-Fuckin'-Nasty, boys. Fucked up, tortured up—sliced and diced. They want the whole Satanic Bill Special."

Klegg let out a laugh. "My pecker is hard thinkin' about it, Bill."

"Well, tell that big guy to stay down. I wouldn't want you tearing through your jeans!" Bill chuckled and then turned back to Chunk and Buster. "This is a major opportunity, fellas. Let's make sure we don't mess it up."

***

Chunk couldn't resist temptation. He stared at the door the whole time and wondered what being with a Faora woman was like. Something made Chunk want to have something special with her.

He'd never had something special one-on-one before.

As soon as Buster fell asleep on the couch, Chunk found himself in Persephone's room. She was so beautiful and innocent-looking. Bill had explained that the women from this community were rare to fuck compared to any old whore off the street. They had pussies made of gold, as he would say.

Chunk proposed a deal to her: if she pleasured him and kept it a secret, she would be rewarded with pizza rolls.

"Now, you better play nice..." he said once again.

"I promise," Persephone urged, locking eyes with Chunk before glancing toward the door. "We won't say a word to anyone else. Our little secret."

She watched as he unzipped his pants and swiftly undid the button. Chunk eagerly stumbled forward, instantly discarding his pants and underwear. He gripped his member tightly and hastily masturbated, trying his best to get hard.

An expression of embarrassment washed over his face. "Apologies. It's just that I'm not accustomed to a woman being so...so..."

"No. Let me. I'll take care of you," she exclaimed, reaching forward with her free hand. Persephone understood that the word Chunk was searching for was "willing."

These ugly, backwoods, inbred boys never had girls wanting them.

Persephone observed him with mixed emotions as he closed his eyes, seemingly lost in a state of pure bliss. At that moment, she held control over him. As Chunk arched his back and emitted grunts of ecstasy, Persephone felt a wave of nausea.

She realized she had to get the rest of her body free, or this would not work. "Um...hey..."

"Yeah?" Chunk asked, opening his eyes and smiling down at her.

"You think you could untie me so I can use both hands?" Persephone asked with a sexual giggle. "It's so big."

Her words seemed to have a magical effect on Chunk as he took the bait. He interrupted her, preventing further action, and reached down to his pants. From his pocket, he retrieved a pocketknife and freed her other arm.

"Feet too?"

Chunk hesitated, and Persephone could tell he was about to say no.

"Our secret," she said in a convincing and seductive tone. "I promise I won't say a word. I want on my knees."

She didn't have to say anything else before Chunk cut the ropes, freeing her legs and radiating excitement.

In an instant, Persephone fell to her knees, her anticipation painted in her wide-eyed gaze. She looked up at Chunk, who loomed above her, his small pulsating member hovering near her mouth. A pungent odor of stale cheese wafted from it, causing her to gag even before parting her lips. Despite her reluctance, Persephone knew she had no choice but to proceed.

Her mouth swiftly engulfed his piece of flesh, sucking it in instantly.

Persephone's stomach churned, a sickening sensation washing over her. The dimly lit room seemed to close in on her as she hesitated, unsure of her actions. But it didn't matter. She had this hillbilly right where she wanted him.

The back left side of her mouth bore the remnants of an accident from her youth, leaving her with jagged teeth. They were sharp enough to dissuade her from pressing her tongue against them too firmly. It was with these teeth that she carried out the unthinkable act of severing his penis from his body.

Persephone swiftly reacted, twisting her body and sinking her teeth into him with all her strength. His head snapped back with a forceful jerk. The action happened in a split second. Blood spattered across her, narrowly missing her eyes. It was like a fountain of crimson expelling from between his legs.

As Persephone turned her gaze toward Chunk, a chilling sight awaited her. His face was drained of color, resembling a ghost, while both of his hands tightly clutched his crotch. The coppery scent of blood filled the air as it cascaded down his legs. His voice failed him, leaving him unable to articulate a single word. In response, Persephone spat a glob of blood at him, and his penis hit the floor. Her grin, tainted with cherry, revealed a fierce side to Persephone.

Chunk shrunk away from her. Persophone could gauge the intensity in her eyes by the fear in his. She understood the power of her glare and relished it as she watched him shake.

Persephone glanced at the floor and noticed the knife he had dropped. Without hesitation, she swiftly retrieved it and rushed at him.

Buster could hear the commotion in the other room and turned down Tom and Jerry to listen. He registered the muffled whales of pain and pondered going inside, unsure if Chunk had started without Bill. The last time his brother didn't listen to Bill's orders, it was not a pleasant sight.

Bill had beaten Chunk within an inch of his life with a tire iron.

Peeling himself from the sofa, Buster stumbled to the door and knocked. The noise stopped, and he couldn't hear anything. If he could talk, he would have. But instead, Buster uttered something only his brothers could understand.

Nothing.

As Buster opened the door, he was greeted with the sight of his brother propped up dead in the room's corner. His throat had been slit several times, along with his wrists, and he had a pool of blood flowing from his legs and crotch.

Buster let out a banshee of a scream. It sounded like a dying animal. His heart sank instantly as he felt a volatile blend of anger and concern. The sight of his big brother, motionless and still, shattered his heart into a million pieces.

He panicked and rushed to Chunk's aid.

He walked right into her trap.

Persophone was perched above the door, holding the heavy chains to the conveyor. She dropped them over his head and caught him by the neck in mid-step. Then, she quickly jumped down, landing on the chain.

Buster didn't have time to react and felt the jerk around his fat neck as his lower body gave from the tension. The trap door beneath him somehow triggered, and he fell through. A pitiful yelp escaped his lips as the chain's slack recoiled against the filthy floor.

Persephone walked to the edge and peered down, searching for where Buster had gone. She found him dangling a few inches above a metal table in the basement. His neck had snapped like a twig.

Two down, she thought, taking a deep breath as she wiped the blood and some pubes from her face. *Just two more to go.*

Satanic Bill fucked up. If he had kidnapped Persephone a few years ago, maybe there would have been a chance for him to succeed. But not now. She was trained for this type of aggression. Everyone in the community was. The Faora Family of Christ's once-nonviolent approach changed after their esteemed elder's passing. The younger leaders took charge and decided they needed to train secretly for the impending apocalypse. *"The world is a dangerous place, and we need to adapt,"* one elder had explained.

Persophones scaled down the chains, using Buster's corpse for a safe landing. After combing the upstairs of the house, she realized the basement would likely be the most fruitful place to find what she was looking for. She could have run away but didn't know her exact location.

Persephone cautiously scanned the basement. She took in all of her surroundings, the gruesome sight of dried blood splattered across the grimy floor and the artwork on the walls. The place made her skin crawl. She knew without a doubt that evil lived there.

She noticed a pile of VHS tapes on one counter by an old box television. Curiosity got the better of her, and she couldn't resist the urge to investigate. Picking up one of the tapes and putting it in the player was a decision she would soon regret. The footage was one of the most depraved things she had ever witnessed.

Persephone knew she had been kidnapped for a reason.

Her mission in life became clear: seek revenge for all the women who had suffered in this house of horrors. Satanic Bill, the true mastermind behind the evil deeds, was the one responsible. Persephone aimed to make him pay.

Bill entered the house, his footsteps crunching on the floor littered with dirt and chicken bones. The absence of

Buster's and Chunk's usually eager barks left a void in the air. They were always ready to shoot the next film when he made them wait too long. He casually tossed the thirty-pack of beer onto the table, resulting in a loud THUD. The impact knocked old food containers to the floor.

He called out for them.

But no answer.

Klegg walked in, his hands full of groceries, and looked around. "Did they pass out or something?" he inquired.

"Something…" Bill said, his head perking up as he sniffed the air, "… feels off." He looked at Klegg and nodded.

Klegg threw the grocery bags on the ground and walked out of the house. Bill pulled a small pistol from his jacket and walked to the living room. He could see the flashing of the television still on around the corner.

His breathing quickened, and a chill crept into his palms. "Chunk! Buster!" he screamed out. "You two bitch hogs better be fuckin' round!"

He turned and slowly entered the living room, feeling his heart pounding in his throat. Bill refused to admit his fear, but deep down, he couldn't deny it.

"What the actual…" He yelled, turning the corner to point his gun in the television's direction. "Ain't no fucking way."

Chunk lay slumped on the worn couch, his discarded pants sprawled beside him. The air in the room was heavy with the metallic stench of blood wafting from his legs and crotch. Bill's gaze fixed on the sight of Chunk's head, tilted unnaturally backward, revealing a grotesque, wide-open neck where it appeared someone had made a gruesome attempt to sever it. A shiver shot down Bill's spine as he noticed a small piece of meat dangling from Chunk's mouth.

Bill quickly realized the chunk of flesh in the boy's mouth was his penis.

"Klegg! Get—"

Bill was suddenly silenced when a hard metal object shot from the darkness and struck him square in the face. His decayed teeth shattered under the force of the blow, and his hat was knocked off his head. In the midst of it all, his finger instinctively squeezed the trigger of the gun. A round pumped out, and he was cracked again with the object.

Losing his balance, Bill crumbled to the floor and ended up shooting himself. His vision blurred as stars danced around, leaving him bewildered as he struggled to understand what had occurred.

A horrible scream filled the air.

Bill turned to it in a disoriented haze. The dim light cast eerie shadows on the walls. Through the gloom, he could make out the faint silhouette of Klegg sprawled on the floor near the entrance to the living room. The sharp odor of gunpowder lingered in the air, a stark reminder of the shot that had just echoed through the house.

Klegg's desperate cries pierced the silence. His voice was filled with agony as he rambled about an unseen force gripping his leg, inflicting excruciating pain.

Bill felt immense pain shoot through his leg. He moved his hand down to feel blood pumping out. "Oh fuck! Oh, shit!"

"Bill. It got me," Klegg screamed out, extending his hand toward Bill from across the room. "It hurts!"

"I'm fucking shot over here! I can't do dick!"

Klegg turned his gaze away from Bill and released a bone-chilling scream of sheer terror.

"Klegg! Klegg!" Bill shouted, feeling himself fade into unconsciousness as blood gushed from his leg. "Wh—what is it?"

Bill was jolted awake, startled by the piercing scream. His head throbbed. It took a moment for his eyes to adjust like a camera struggling to focus. The room looked like a chaotic mix of shapes and colors.

A cacophony of loud music and more screaming filled the room. Bill panicked to get his eyes to focus. He wanted to rub them, but something about his body wasn't working.

Amidst the confusion, Bill made out a silhouette of a naked woman standing near a body. As the infectious melody began, the music infiltrated his mind with the opening lines of "The Safety Dance" by Men Without Hats.

Bill loved this song.

But, at the moment, it scared the living shit out of him. His limbs felt numb, and his heart thrummed in utter fear.

The naked woman approached him with a long, sharp blade held by her side. His vision slowly returned, but Bill still felt like he was drowning in a sea of confusion. He looked at his leg. A belt was firmly fastened around his upper thigh, but blood caked the surrounding floor.

"You bled like a stuck pig. It's a good thing I know how to stop wounds like that from bleeding. Needed you around just a little longer." Persephone said, hunching down beside him. "You are a bad man, Bill."

Tears welled up in his eyes, blurring his vision, as he glanced across the room and caught sight of Klegg. But it was no longer the Klegg he knew. The agonizing screams that had filled the air had come from him, and it seemed they had been his final cries. Bound to the "kill chair," Klegg sat lifeless, his breath forever stilled. Strips of his flesh had been meticulously peeled away, exposing raw muscle and bone. The room was drenched in blood. Persephone had transformed Klegg's body into a twisted masterpiece, skillfully carving and shaping it to her mind's desires.

"What...what are you?" he stammered. "You ain't no bitch I ever seen before."

She straddled him, her breasts pressing against his face, causing him to cry out in pain as her weight bore down on his leg. "I'm special, remember?"

"You are one twisted bitch."

"And you, Bill, will scream like a little bitch until your dying breath," she playfully said, poking his nose.

He had no choice but to sit there helplessly as she straddled him. Persephone set the knife aside and reached over Bill, rummaging on the metal table. Finding what she was looking for, she dangled it in Bill's face—a wire garrote.

Bill's eyes widened.

Persephone swiftly wrapped the wire around his neck, extending the two handles to their maximum length without delay.

"Smile, Bill," she exclaimed, her voice filled with excitement, as she nodded toward the corner.

Bill's eyes followed her gaze to a video camera. Its red light blinked steadily, almost mocking him with its eerie glow. His trembling lips managed to form a pitiful smile as the metal wire dug into his flesh. She was going to take his head clean off.

This was gonna be a Full Nasty for sure!

Turduckin'
Sidney Shiv

When Skeet Morrisette told the bitch he was going to eat her pussy, he found it hilarious when she didn't realize he wasn't *'spittin' purdy in-yer-endo'* at her.

Skeet picked her up at the Blind Beacon truck stop on route three. It took him a few minutes to browse three of four meth-mouthed skanks before he found her—a nice, plump young thing with a fat dumper. She was as fresh a piece of rent-a-pussy as he ever lay eyes on. He pulled his old pickup to the far end of the lot, where she leaned against the wall of the self-service car wash, rolled his window down, and waved her over.

She strutted to the truck, the bottom of her milkers hanging from a halter top cut just below the nip line. Her Levi cut-offs left nothing to the imagination. If they rode any higher, the pucker of her balloon knot would be on display for every swinging dick in Dent County. Skeet's rod stirred, and his gut growled. *Horney and hungry at the same time*, he thought. *I guess I'm* Horngry!

"Hiya, Sweetness," he said, greeting her jovially. "How much?"

She pressed her titties through his open window and pulled a lollipop out of her cock-sucker with a popping sound, licking her lips. "Twenty-five for a handy, fifty for a blowy, seventy-five for some pussy, and a hundred will getcha some asshole."

"A hunnert will get me everything—blow job, pussy, and ass?" Skeet asked. He wanted it all.

"If you want, I can give you some pussy and ass for a hundred. If you want a suck-off first, that'll be a hundred-n-twenty. That'll getcha 'round the world." She slid the lollipop back into her pouty gob and raised her eyebrows questioningly.

Skeet took his John Deere cap off and ran a hand through his greasy brown hair, whistling—a bit of showmanship for the bargaining tango they were engaged in. Of course, he knew the cunt wouldn't be getting one red cent. But the offer had to sound legit if he wanted to get her in the truck. "A hunnert-n-twenty for a trip 'round the world, you say? That's a bit steep for my blood. Keep in mind, you'll be getting something out of the deal, too—besides just money, I mean."

Her eyes narrowed. The sucker made clickety-clack sounds as she rolled it around in her cheek. "Oh yeah? And what would that be?"

Skeet flashed his best Elvis Presley smile and winked, pouring on the charm. He slowly looked her up and down, scanning the length of her body, and said, "Darlin', yer purdier than a shiny new flywheel. You've never known a fuckin' like the one I'm about to treat that clam-a-yers to. I'll eat that pussy to smithereens and suck a turd straight outta yer asshole. You'll come yourself retarded by the time I'm through with your sweet chocolate ass. I'm gonna fuck you longer, harder, and freakier than your favorite uncle ever did. So, what do you say? A hunnert fer 'round the world?"

The skank seemed unmoved by his proposition. She popped the sucker from her mouth again. "I told you my prices. Take 'em or leave 'em. But hurry up and make up your mind. There're other tricks I could be servicing while we stand here jawin'."

This fuckin' bitch, he thought. *She's gonna be a tough nut to crack.* He felt his dick grow another inch. His mind reeled with the images of all the tasty fun he could have with her. After squeezing off his first round in her, he'd open her wide and watch her bleed out. Then he'd sink his teeth into her warm, sweaty flesh and sate his other appetite. Once he'd savored a small appetizer, he'd fuck every piece of the whore's carcass all livelong day—rinse and repeat. "Okay, then. A hunnert-n-twenty it is. You drive a hard bargain."

She smirked as if she'd known all along that she'd get what she wanted. "You can call me Leena. I've got a room across the street at the Super 8 Motel. Let's head on over and get this party started."

Skeet feigned surprise. "Hold up just a second. I can't go to the motel. Too many people in this town would recognize my truck in the parkin' lot. I'm a happily married man. Can't risk it gettin' back to my wife if someone saw me there—no siree! That would open a whole can of worms. How about we go camping? I got a nice spot picked out—"

"No deal," Leena cut him off, turning to walk away.

"Wait! Hold up!" Skeet called after her, seeing the distance grow between himself and his evening smorgasbord. "Here's twenty bucks. Just hear me out, and if you still don't like the deal, you can walk away twenty bucks richer." He held out a twenty-dollar bill.

She turned back to the truck and snatched the twenty out of his hand.

That's right, fishy! Green is like stink bait to every whore.

"Now just listen—" *What the fuck did she say her name was?* "—Leena. I've got a nice campsite picked out at Locust Forrest National Park, just up the road. I figured we'd camp, party, and just hang out for the night. I've got hotdogs, beer, and a boombox with every CD Johnny Paycheck ever put out. I'll have you back here bright and early tomorrow morning. I promise I ain't no psycho killer."

Leena sighed. "Even if I wanted to, I couldn't. I'd be missing out on too much money from other tricks," she said.

Skeet could tell he was whittling away her reservations. He laughed and rolled his eyes, acting like the most innocent of silly gooses. "Is that all this is about? Money?" He pulled a thick wad of cash out of his pocket and theatrically thumbed the bills. "Okay, then. I'll give you five-hunnert for the night."

As he watched her big doe eyes zero in on the cash, he knew he had her—hook, line, and sinker.

After staring at the bills, Leena returned her gaze to him, her expression hardening. "I usually make twice that in a night."

Skeet knew he had to finesse this portion of the transaction just right. She had to believe she would be walking away with his hard-earned money. If he immediately gave in to whatever price she set, she'd be suspicious he was conning her. He could have easily said, "Here's a thousand! No, make it two thousand—now hop in the truck!" But she would have seen right through that. If he continued haggling down like he was on a budget and fixing to part with a large sum of money, then she would trust he was an innocent workin' Joe just trying to get a little stink on his dick.

"That may be true," Skeet admitted. "But how many pokes do you have to take per night to make a thousand? For five-hunnert, all you have to deal with is me. And, like I said, I plan on treating that pussy right. The rest of the time, we can hang out, drink some beer, eat some dogs, and listen to some tunes. It'll be like a mini vacation."

Skeet could see the wheels spinning in her hooker brain as he watched her practically drool over his stack of cash. He decided to drive the nail in her coffin, thumbing the wad one more time before sticking it in the breast pocket of his flannel shirt. Her eyes betrayed a brief flash of longing as the money disappeared. "So, what'll it be, darlin'? Make up yer mind. A fun camping trip and the fuck of your life with me, or five to ten stinky trucker dicks at the Super 8? Clocks-a-tickin, Sweetheart. I know what I'd choose—unless, of course, you enjoy the flavor of smegma. If you don't wanna come, I'm sure some other purdy piece around here will jump at the proposition. Hell, I might not even have to spend five-hunnert."

Leena stood silently with an expression of deep appraisal. Then she threw her sucker on the ground and sighed like she knew she was making the biggest mistake of her life. "Okay. Let's do this," she said and ran around to the passenger side of the truck, her bulbous chest ornaments bouncing like water balloons.

She got in and sat her delicious ass down on the bench seat beside him. "And what should I call you, Cowboy?"

He looked at her and smiled. "The name's Scott Morrissette. But you can call me Skeet."

"Don't be spittin'. You swallow that shit, Daisy. Tricks will likely come back for more if they be thinkin' you dig their flavor." EZ Sleaze loved turning out new bitches, breaking them in before putting them to work.

Daisy gulped, batting her eyelashes. She licked her lips and opened her mouth to show it was empty. Her creamy Asian skin glowed in the soft red lighting of EZ's bedroom.

EZ sat up in his king-size bed. "Good girl," he said, running his hand down her thigh. "You ready to earn?"

"Yeah, Daddy. I'm ready. Let's make some fucking cash!" Daisy said, her little titties jiggling as she bounced excitedly on the bed.

"All right. Now, I've given you the price breakdown. Today is Saturday. When do you pay me?" EZ's expression became serious as he quizzed her.

"Friday afternoon," she answered.

"How much do you pay me each week?" he asked.

"One thousand dollars," she replied.

"That's right. That may seem like a lot, but if you hustle, you can clear that on a busy Friday night. Some of my hoes pull in three to five G's a week. That's a lot of horny dicks, but it's all about how bad you want it. Either way, I get mine—a thousand a week. That pays for your room at the 8 and protection. Five hundred of what you pay me goes to Amir, the motel manager. If you get into a scrape, you call me. My house is right behind the motel. I can be there on foot in less than a minute. If I can't get there quick enough, I call Amir, and he'll be there in an instant to cool a mother fucker out."

"What kind of scrapes are you talking about?" Daisy asked.

"The kind of scrapes where a trick might act a fool trying to take something you ain't offering. Just 'cause you a hoe don't mean you ain't got limits. You're down to fuck.

Beyond that, you decide what they can and can't do with you."

"Do they get violent very often when they don't get what they want?"

"There were a few incidents when we first set up shop." EZ slid a hair pick into his afro, then ran his fingers down the sides of his goatee. "But after Amir and I dealt a few ass-beatings, word circulated that if you fucked around, you'd find out. Nowadays, the clientele is relatively docile. Every once in a while, a mother fucker steps out of line and gets served. That's just the cost of doing business."

"So sexy. I feel warm and safe knowing Daddy has my back," She ran her hand up EZ's thigh.

"Chill, bitch," EZ said, grabbing her wrist. "I'm almost fifty. I'm lucky to get one good nut a day. Any more than that, and my Johnson's blowing bubbles. Besides, you need to get to work—start earning us that green."

Daisy huffed and began milling around the bedside for her clothes. She yanked up a pair of short shorts, then pulled a tank top over her head. Her nipples poked through the fabric like a pair of Hershey's Kisses.

"Oh, I almost forgot..." EZ swung his legs out of bed and reached for his nightstand drawer. He rummaged around for a moment, then turned to face her. "This is for you."

He handed her a little black disk about the size of a nickel and twice as thick. Daisy turned it between her fingers, examining it with wonder. She looked quizzically at EZ.

"That's a GPS tracker. I use them to keep track of all my hoes. You keep it on you, always—either in a pocket or taped to the inside of a belt...whatever. I need to know where you are at all times. I don't give a fuck what you're doing or what day it is. You better have this with you as long as you work for me. Don't let me find out you're leavin' it places where you ain't. I don't play with no triflin'-ass skanks. If you decide you don't wanna work for me anymore, that's cool. We'll go our separate ways, no static. But as long as you're my bitch, you will keep this tracker on your person. And if you decide to leave the compound—the immediate area of the truck stop, the motel, and my house—call and let me know what's up so I know you're safe. Understand?"

She giggled. "Of course, Daddy. I don't care if you know where I am. I like it. It makes me feel safe." She buttoned her shorts and tucked the tracker into her pocket.

EZ rummaged through his drawer again and withdrew a key attached to a plastic, diamond-shaped tag. He handed it to Daisy. "Here you go. All yours. Room twenty-eight. Amir gives us a quiet block of rooms at the end of the row—Marla's in twenty-six. Leena's next to you in twenty-seven, and Cinnamon is on your other side in twenty-nine. They are there for you as well if you need anything. You ladies have to look out for each other. You've met them, right?"

"Yeah. Dre Quan introduced me to them," Daisy replied.

"Well, bully for Dre. He did right by bringing you to me. We are going to do well together, I can tell. Now, get your tight little ass to work."

EZ watched as Daisy finished buckling the straps of her high heels and then stood, grabbing her leopard print purse from the nightstand. She kissed his cheek and waved as she exited the bedroom. A moment later, he heard the front door shut as she walked out.

EZ grabbed his phone from the nightstand and opened the tracking app. He clicked Daisy's icon and watched the little dot slowly move around the map of his block, heading for the motel. "Bye, hoe. It's off to work, you go," he muttered, hearing the tune from the Disney movie.

EZ clicked on Cinnamon's icon. According to her tracker, she was in the Blind Beacon lot, across the street from the motel. He clicked on Marla's icon. She appeared to be in her room at the motel. Leena's icon was last. "What the fuck!" he yelled.

Zooming out on the map, the streets of downtown Dentsville appeared like varicose veins on the cottage cheese ass of Dent County. The dots representing the whereabouts of Daisy, Marla, and Cinnamon were tightly grouped like a cluster of warts on that ass—where they were supposed to be. Not Leena, though. No—that bitch was way the fuck out in the boonies of the county like a lone herpes sore. He zoomed in and squinted. Her dot wasn't even near a road. It was alone in the middle of a green patch of nothing, at least twenty miles outside the city.

She'd better be in some shit, he thought as he got up to get dressed. *They know they need to tell me if they go off the reservation. Otherwise, how am I supposed to know whether or not some fool threw them into the trunk and lit the fuck out?*

After EZ donned his black tracksuit, he went to his closet and grabbed his oldest pair of Jordans. He didn't know what type of terrain he was headed into and didn't want to risk ruining one of his more expensive pairs. Either way, that bitch was going to pay for them if they got fucked up.

His last order of business before heading out was grabbing the Glock 22 from his nightstand drawer. He released the magazine and checked to make sure it was fully loaded.

After slamming it back into the weapon's grip, he pulled the slide back enough to reveal a .40 caliber round in the chamber without ejecting it.

Locked and loaded, he thought. *This is a fucked up way to spend a Saturday night. Leena, you'd better be in trouble. If you're dragging me out of my crib, I better get to make Swiss cheese out of a mother fucker. But if this is some bullshit, I'll be paddling that ass.*

"Goddamn it, fuck!" Leena said, scowling at her cell phone.

"What?" Skeet asked, glancing at her from the driver's seat.

"I forgot, I needed to make a call before we rolled out. Now I don't have any service." She looked out the passenger window. On the right side of the road was a vast expanse of freshly planted corn fields as far as the eye could see. Small clusters of buildings dotted the landscape of gently rolling hills, each consisting of a white farmhouse, red barn, and silos. *Like something out of an Edward Hicks painting*, Leena thought.

"Service probably won't be any better where we're headed," Skeet commented.

"That's all right," Leena sighed. She'd explain it all to EZ tomorrow. He'd understand if she slipped him an extra hundred.

Leena gazed past Skeet out the driver's side of the truck. Tall deciduous trees, heavy with springtime foliage, formed a completely different landscape on the other side of the road. It was as if they traveled along an unseen boundary between worlds with rich rolling farmland to the north and dark forested foothills to the south. The setting sun melting into the blacktop miles ahead only emphasized the divide.

As the golden orb dipped below the horizon, leaving a trail of bloodstained ozone as a reminder of its existence, Skeet turned the truck off the main road. Leena bid the waning daylight farewell as she allowed herself to be swallowed up, alongside this stranger, by the all-consuming maw of trees.

"Almost there, Sugar-tits," Skeet said, moving his right hand from the gear shifter to his groin.

"Hell yeah, Daddy. You gonna treat this pussy right?" Leena responded, getting into character. She turned toward him, running her hands seductively up her abdomen, and popped her left breast out from under her high-riding halter top. After giving her nipple a quick tweak, she covered it back up.

"Oh, Mamma," Skeet said, smiling like a donkey.

Leena could see his mouth glistening, even in the dark. She watched him lick his lips with a slurping sound as he stared at her tits. He wiped his mouth with his forearm, turning back to the road. *Did that motherfucker just drool*, she wondered.

They drove past a decrepit sign reading LOCUST FOREST NATIONAL PARK. A moment later, they approached a small gate booth in a median between the incoming and outgoing lanes. Leena looked left to see if a park ranger was working the booth. She only saw cobwebs and an unoccupied chair inside the vestibule as they passed.

"They ain't had a ranger working the park since the pandemic. I guess Uncle Sam liked the money he was savin' and decided to keep it that way once people were allowed back into the world," Skeet said.

"Interesting," Leena replied, doing her best to fake interest. She felt a tingle of alienation at the idea of no rangers patrolling the park, but the irony wasn't lost on her. In the urban areas, surrounded by people, she fought to avoid any legal authorities like the plague. But out here, surrounded by miles of nothing on all sides, it would have been a comfort to believe that some anonymous force was proactively working in the interest of her well-being.

Leena remembered the GPS chip EZ had given her. She doubted he would be on his way out to East Jesus or where ever the fuck this was to check on her welfare. It was Saturday night, and he was training a new girl. If he noticed she was gone, she'd probably get slapped around for her indiscretion when she returned. If this Skeet character turned out to be a serial killer, EZ might have an *easier* time locating her body if he felt so inclined. *Hurray technology!*

"Well, I like it," Skeet remarked, staring at the forest. "Ever since they pulled the funding, the place has been quiet—no fuck face tourists milling around with their screaming kids or smokey the bear stormtroopers monitoring the height of your campfires. Now, it's gone back to nature—a place where discerning adults can engage in primal activities without fear of Johnny Law dipping his fat beak in. It's as it should be—as God intended."

Great, Leena thought. *I'm stuck miles out in the middle of nowhere with the Henry David Thoreau of pussy hounds.* If she could make it through one more year of working for EZ, she'd be able to pay for college and begin a new life as a teacher in a faraway place where no one knew what she had to do to achieve those goals. *One thing at a time,* she thought. *Let's focus on making it through the night with this weirdo first.*

After driving several miles into the deserted park, Skeet pulled off into the small parking lot of a trailhead. He reached across Leena, grabbed a flashlight from the glove box, and got out of the truck. She followed.

They hiked into the woods for what seemed like ages, Skeet leading the way with the flashlight. Leena tried paying attention to her surroundings in case she needed to find her way out alone but quickly gave up. The darkness made her efforts futile. She was angry for having placed herself in such a precarious position. *Goddamn greed made me forget the first rule,* she thought. *Never go against your gut.*

Leena clutched her purse. The small can of pepper spray inside was her insurance policy. She would remain vigilant, resigning herself to whatever the evening held in store.

"Here we are," Skeet announced as they entered a small clearing. He shined the flashlight on the campsite. A small tent, two folding chairs, a cooler, and a portable boombox were positioned around a freshly made firepit. "I set up camp earlier today. Beer's in the cooler. Help yourself. I'll get the fire started."

Leena sighed, beginning to feel more at ease. She went to the cooler and opened it. Bottles of beer were packed in ice on one side, and a pack of hotdogs and condiments occupied the other. "You want one, too," Leena asked.

"Hell yeah," Skeet replied as he knelt before the pyramid of firewood. He flicked his lighter, igniting the dry leaves and kindling in the center. As the flame grew, he stood and turned toward Leena.

"Here you go, Sugar," she said, handing him the beer. She twisted the top off of hers.

"Cheers," he said, opening his and tapping the neck of his bottle with hers. He chugged his beer thirstily.

Leena also drank deeply. The hike had been sweaty work, and the beer tasted great. She was glad she'd never been one for high heels, opting for more comfortable footwear. It was a mystery to her that so many others in her line of work would wear such unconventional shoes when the job demanded hours of standing outside.

Skeet drained his bottle. He belched and wiped his mouth when he finished, leering at her strangely. The horney bastard seemed to be appraising her. The way his eyes lingered, and his lips glistened, he appeared...*hungry*. She felt like a sirloin on his dinner plate.

He threw his empty bottle into the woods. It landed with a hollow thump in the darkness. A commotion of quick footfall and snapping twigs ignited out of sight in the underbrush.

"What the fuck was that?" Leena said, turning to the darkness outside the camp's perimeter.

"Just an animal—a rabbit, or possum, or some shit," Skeet said and laughed. "The only animal you have to worry about out here is me." He made a growling sound and raised his hands in a claw-like pantomime.

Leena shrugged. "Okay. Fuck you then, possum!" She chugged the rest of her beer and threw the bottle into the darkness.

"Atta girl! You ready to get this party started?" Skeet asked. He went to the tent and unzipped the flap. Holding it open with one hand, he bowed and made an ushering gesture with the other, like a butler.

Skeet shined the flashlight as she crouched to enter the tent. A sleeping bag was spread on the floor. As she lowered herself to her knees, she noticed a grocery bag containing hotdog buns and what appeared to be the fixings for smores. Her tension eased a little more. So far, Skeet seemed on the level—a little strange, but on the level. She clutched her purse nonetheless.

The flashlight's beam danced haphazardly as Skeet zipped the tent flap. Crouching, he turned and hung the flashlight from a hook in the center of the tent's ceiling, then went to his knees in front of her. He wasted no time.

Leena let out a surprised squeak as Skeet ran his hands up her hips. They glided over her ribs before landing beneath her breasts, cupping them. She dropped her purse as he pulled her shirt over her head. She'd scarcely finished shaking the halter top off her arms when he lunged at her breasts, hungrily sucking and nibbling on each in turn.

"Okay," she said, reveling in his gusto. It wasn't often that a John paid any attention to her pleasure. She unzipped his fly and pushed his jeans and boxers down. An instant later, she had his hard length in the palm of her hand. It flexed as she stroked it. The sheer girth and above-average length of his cock sent a tingle of anticipation into her pussy.

Skeet took his shirt off, then sat down and pulled his pants the rest of the way off. She did the same. When they were naked, he pulled her on top of him in the sixty-nine position.

Leena was taken aback by the skill with which he ate her pussy. Not many Johns would take such a chance on hooker poon. Not only was Skeet paying ample attention to her clit, but he was sucking her labia and licking inside the hole. *Good Lord,* she thought a moment later as he began licking her asshole. When he pressed his finger into her anus, she took his shaft in her mouth and swallowed it to the hilt. *This mother fucker may earn himself two trips 'round the world.*

She turned around and straddled him, inserting his thick rod. It went in slow. His glans was the size of an apple, and taking it into her vagina was like giving birth in reverse. When the head of his dick finally disappeared into her, the girthy shaft followed with relative ease.

Her pussy gushed at the sensation of being filled to the brim. Slow, deliberate thrusts became fast and fierce as her pussy slickened. The walls of her vagina ballooned as a torrent of sex juice sprayed with her orgasm. She'd never squirted before and was shocked by the speed and ferocity of her orgasm.

Lina lifted herself. Skeet's dick slapped to his belly. She gripped it and repositioned herself over him, aiming his tool at her asshole. Slowly, she eased herself onto it, knowing she wouldn't shit right for a month when all was said and done. *Fuck it.* He'd earned it. And she was enjoying herself just as much as he was, maybe more.

As she continued riding him, she glanced at her purse beside her. Better safe than sorry. Everything seemed to be going well, but it was nice knowing the pepper spray was there—just in case. It also helped that she knew where his hands were as they roved her flesh.

Skeet groped her tits with both hands, twisting and pinching her nipples. She took one of his hands and guided it to her pussy. Leaning back, she pressed his fingers into her gauged-out sex. He took the hint and fist-fucked her as she slammed her ass on his cock.

Skeet's breathing became heavy. That drooling, hungry look came over his face again. Leena supposed he was about to bust his nut and marveled at how everyone she'd encountered had a different orgasm expression.

Skeet shivered and took his hand off her breast, lowering it to his side. "I'm going to tear that nipple off with my teeth and swallow it whole as I drink the blood from your tit!" he growled, thrusting beneath her.

"Come again?" she said, still riding him.

Skeet howled, bucking beneath her in orgasm. "I'm going stuff the end of your intestines into your fuck hole and squeeze the shit into your box like toothpaste."

"That's some strange pillow talk, Sugar," Leena said, reaching for her purse. One of his hands was still lodged in her pussy, but Leena could tell he was rooting around under the side of the sleeping bag with the other. "What are you looking for?" she asked, finding the pepper spray.

"Die bitch!" Skeet screamed as he sat up, pulling a large hunting knife out from under the sleeping bag.

Leena raised the pepper spray in time to see a brown shaft pierce the side of the tent and plunge into Skeet's eye. Skeet released a surprised squeak as he dropped the knife and fell back. As the first spear retracted from his eye socket with a wet sucking sound, another pierced the canvas wall and found his throat.

"What the fu—" Leena's last words were cut short as a wooden spike entered her back and blasted out through her left tit, piercing her heart and obliterating her nipple. Another spear pierced the tent, entering her torso. A final lance found her thigh.

Each wooden spear exited her flesh with a zipping sound as they were pulled, one by one, through the tent walls. She fell back with Skeet's fist still in her pussy. Leena pondered one last dying question as she bled out: *Was 'Die bitch' the best you could come up with, Skeet?*

EZ Sleaze pulled his lime green 73 Caprice into the layby and parked beside a beat-up pickup truck—the only other vehicle in the lot. He'd found the turn for Locust Forrest National Park easy enough. Judging by the tracker, it was the only viable option between downtown Dentsville and Lake Orange.

During the ride, he'd tried calling Leena several times. As each call was directed immediately to voicemail, his level of pissed-off was gradually replaced with concern. Halfway to the park, his cell service shit the bed. *Maybe that's all it is,* he thought. *She came out here for one reason or another, tried to call, and lost service. Makes sense.*

EZ almost turned back and headed for home but decided to stay the course. He knew a good pimp would only remain a good pimp if he maintained control of his bitches. This meant knowing where they were and overseeing their safety. Besides, he was interested in discovering what was so important that it could drag his best hoe all the way out to Bum-fucksville. If something dubious had occurred, he'd step in and represent. If her reasons were monetary, he had a vested interest in securing his piece of the pie.

He grabbed his Glock and a flashlight from the glove box. After exiting his ride, he tucked the gun in his waistband and turned on the flashlight. Peering into the locked pickup didn't offer any clues about Leena's situation, so he proceeded to the trail.

Though the cell service was shit, the tracker app still worked. The dot was about a quarter of a mile south as the crow flies. He knew it wouldn't be wise to try hiking a straight line for it. That would take him off the trail, and he was uncertain of the terrain, especially in the dark. He'd stay on the path as long as possible before veering into the wild.

The trees swayed ominously. The breeze hissing through the leaves almost sounded like rushing water. EZ was a city person and not used to the sounds of nature. He heard wood creak as it bent to the wind's will. The crunch of dead leaves and skittering in the distance startled him. He felt his nut skin tighten as he reached for his piece.

"Fuckin' squirrels," EZ muttered. Something called through the darkness as if in response. It was like a mix between a howl and a monkey laughing. The unexpected sound traveled across the forest floor as its unseen maker moved in the distance. EZ only caught sight of tree trunks and blackness as he quickly panned his light. He froze, his heart hammering in his chest, waiting to hear if anything was creeping in his direction. Nothing. Shaking it off, he kept moving.

After walking for what felt like hours, he came to a spot where it seemed like remaining on the trail would circle him back to the parking area rather than get him closer to Leena. He knew it was time to abandon the trail and make a beeline for the dot. EZ looked at the tracker app and oriented himself, making sure he was pointed in the right direction. According to the app, Leena was only a couple hundred yards away. He slid his phone in his pocket. "Here we go," he said as he stepped off the trail.

EZ turned off his flashlight and allowed his eyes to adjust to the darkness, treading as quietly as possible. Maintaining a stealthy advantage would be advantageous if Leena was in a bad situation. Hopefully, he'd find everything copacetic, but better safe than sorry.

After several minutes of creeping slowly and quietly through the trees, he caught sight of something. As he moved, an orange glow twinkled in and out of view from behind the black silhouettes of trees ahead. Eventually, he drew close enough to walk a clear line toward it. He stopped when he realized the glow was the dying embers of a campfire.

As he listened for Leena's voice or any signs of what was happening, he heard nothing. EZ proceeded forward, keeping his light off. He quickly assessed his surroundings, ready to seek cover behind the nearest tree at the first sign of someone hearing his approach. He shifted his flashlight to his left hand and drew his gun with his right.

Making his way into the murky campsite, he discovered he was alone. He turned on the flashlight and surveyed the scene. A cooler lay tipped on its side with a half-melted heap of ice fanned in the dirt. The shredded remains of a tent were sprawled haphazardly a few feet away.

EZ tucked his gun back into his waistband as he approached the flattened tent. He knelt and lifted a flap of the torn canvass. The coppery scent hit him as his flashlight illuminated the syrupy red mess coating the tent's interior. "Mother fucker," he whispered, recognizing Leena's purse among a jumble of clothes and a blood-soaked sleeping bag.

EZ rose and turned, shining the light full circle as he drew his gun. As he scoured his surroundings, he caught sight of bloody drag marks in the dirt leading from the tent into the forest. He aimed the flashlight beam and his gun in the same direction.

Leaves rustled, and twigs snapped out of sight. As EZ trained the beam of his flashlight, struggling to see into the woods, the howling, monkey laughter returned. His spine tingled, knowing that whoever *or whatever* was out there could see him, but he couldn't see them. He also realized this culprit was responsible for whatever bloody massacre had occurred inside the tent.

"I see you, mother fucker!" EZ lied. "You fucked with my best hoe. Now you gonna pay!" He fired three shots into the darkness, hoping to scare the individual off long enough to get the fuck out.

When the gunshots' ringing faded from his ears, the insidious laughter began again. A moment later, another giggle of the same ilk echoed to the left, and two more followed suit to the right. In short order, an unseen cacophony of animalistic laughter surrounded him.

EZ's shoulders slumped as the Glock and flashlight dropped to his sides. Fear like he'd never known pounded through his veins as he waited. He barely had time to register the quick patter of running feet behind him before a blow to the back of his head rendered him unconscious.

As his vision came into focus, EZ realized he was naked and sitting in a lawn chair. A similar chair was positioned across from him. His wrists and ankles were bound tightly in twine. He could hear voices speaking and various commotions occurring around him. The back of his head throbbed as he lifted it to look around.

He found himself in a sizable clearing on the side of a tree-covered foothill. A bonfire illuminated the area in wavering titian light. The fire was flanked on both sides by thick wooden y-posts. On one side of the clearing sat the ruins of an old building, perhaps a church. Nothing remained of the structure except a leering façade backed by three crumbling walls. The façade was about twenty feet tall, while the remains of the other walls were no higher than three feet. Across the bonfire, on the other side of the clearing, a tall tree stood out against the surrounding forest. Its gnarly shape and the out-of-season hue of its golden leaves gave it an otherworldly appearance.

Naked men and women milled around the clearing. A cluster of maybe ten toiled near the campfire. EZ couldn't tell what they were doing, but some were down on their knees working on something while others stood around staring and directing. Shitty country music was playing on a boombox.

"What the fuck?" EZ muttered.

As the nude clearing dwellers turned their attention to him, EZ was seized by a new wave of terror. The men looked like humans, but their faces were eerily rodential. Their eyes were solid black dots, void of emotion. They cast maniacal, buck-tooth grins through cleft upper lips. Greyish-brown fuzz coated the bodies of males and females alike.

One of them ran to EZ—a female, judging by her breasts and lack of a penis. He squirmed as she sniffed at his face. Raising his bound hands, he feebly tried to ward her off. She giggled insanely, ignoring his protests and running her foul tongue up his cheek. The stench wafting off of her fur-matted body was a bouquet of cow shit and ass sweat.

The humanoid she-rodent backed off and hurried away, disappearing behind the façade of the ruined church. As EZ looked around, stunned, the eyes of the other rat people returned to their tasks. He thought about breaking his binds and making a run for it but knew they'd be on him the moment he tried.

After a few minutes, a woman emerged from the doorway of the ruins. Unlike the others, she didn't display any rodentlike characteristics. Her red hair hung over her naked breasts, and her pale skin glowed like the moon. The rat-girl followed closely behind, then veered off to return to her duties.

The red-haired woman sat across from EZ in the second lawn chair. She cradled a possum like a baby in the crook of her arm. When she raised the critter to her breast, it suckled.

EZ stared, speechless.

The woman smiled at EZ. "Why are you here?" she asked gently.

"I—uh—I came to check up on my hoe," EZ stammered. "I found a campsite...a tent...blood..."

The woman's gaze remained soft as she regarded him quizzically. "*Hoe?* What is this *hoe* you speak of?"

EZ trembled with fear and awe. "Leena...She's my bitch...I'm her pimp—her boss. I think she came out here to fuck, and I wanted to make sure she was safe."

An expression of understanding lit the woman's face. "Ah...this Leena is a whore, and you are her master."

"I guess you could put it that way," EZ replied.

The woman stroked the possum nursing at her tit. "The universe is made of an infinite number of cycles—cycles of nature, cycles of violence, cycles of love. These cycles are not only linked but woven together like chainmail. For some, this chainmail girds against the stones and pikes of adversity. Others find themselves dragged down by its weight into the bog of loathing and despair. In my existence, I've stood victorious and been vindicated behind the armor. I've also drowned under its burden."

"Who are you? What is this place?" EZ asked, not understanding her words.

"I am bound to this land and this land to me. These are my children. Once a year, during the spring equinox, I permit them to return to human form—well, almost." She smiled at her opossum. "Little Jack remains quite content as a possum. He's a singular and special soul. But the rest are happy to take human form and feast."

"A feast?" EZ asked.

The woman nodded. "Even the damned deserve the occasional reprieve. They usually hunt deer and rabbits. This year, however, nature has seen fit to offer them a strange bounty."

EZ gulped. "What would that be?"

"See for yourself," she said, gesturing toward the bonfire.

EZ turned his head. His jaw dropped at the sight. Two bodies were trussed like turkeys, chests facing up, their arms tied behind their backs, their legs bent and fastened to their chests. They were lined up, one behind the other. EZ could tell they'd been gutted and crudely stitched back together. Spriggs of herbs poked sloppily out from between the widely spaced sutures.

Though headless and genderless, the first body appeared to be a white male. EZ knew the second was Leena. Her chocolate skin and ample breasts gave her away. Her head was intact, but it had been inserted into the hollowed-out ass cavity of the white man's body. A hefty wooded spit, at least twenty feet long, impaled them both. It entered through her gaping posterior, ran the length of her spine, out her mouth, through his body, and out between his headless shoulders.

Even in his utter abhorrence, a funny thought occurred to EZ. He recalled one Thanksgiving when his uncle Omar made a turducken—a chicken stuffed inside a duck stuffed inside a turkey. *What a funny word,* he thought. *This dude's a* turd, *and that bitch loves* fuckin'*—turduckin.'*

Four rodent men, two on each end, lifted the spit. They worked as a unit, communicating in a chittery language EZ didn't recognize. The sturdy bough hardly bent under the weight of their dubious feast as they prepared to hoist the spit onto the y-posts flanking the fire.

"Halt, children," the woman called.

The four men maneuvering the spit paused and directed their beady gazes at the woman.

"Make room for one more," the woman ordered.

As the men lowered the spit to the ground, a few others approached EZ.

"Why?" he asked, tears stinging his eyes. "What did I do?"

The woman's countenance became stern. "Those others became fair game for my children the moment they fornicated on our land. You—as her whore master—are connected to them and therefore share in their guilt."

One of the men pulled EZ out of the chair by his ankle binds and dragged him to the strange tree at the edge of the clearing. Under the tree, they looped a slipknot around his feet. As they tightened the knot, he noticed a glistening tangle of bloody entrails next to him.

A moment later, EZ was lifted off the ground by his ankles. When his head was about two feet high, the other end of the rope was secured, and he dangled helplessly over the pile of guts. As he hung there, he pondered the many cycles of the universe—in particular, the cycle of pimp, hooker, and John—and resigned himself to his rightful place on the spit with his head up Leena's twat-cavity.

EZ laughed out loud as the blade zipped through his abdomen. As his innards sloshed past his face, the final thing to go through his mind tickled him to the core. *It could be worse,* he thought as his vision faded. *I could be the one in the middle.*

You Have a New Message
DE McCluskey

Clive pressed the send button. His heart was thundering so loud he could hear it bouncing around his head and thumping in his ears. The sweet rush of adrenaline made what he was doing, what he loved to do, so worthwhile. He clicked off the social media site he was logged onto. He had so many profiles on so many different platforms that, sometimes, it confused him.

He put himself away, buttoned up his jeans, and stood up.

Grinning, he walked away from his screen, safe in the knowledge that another unsuspecting victim would be waking up to a high-definition, close-up picture of his flaccid penis.

It was truly the best part of his day. He was ready to be inundated with an influx of hate mail, messages telling him to kill himself, messages telling him the disgusting picture would be forwarded all over the internet, naming and shaming him. He loved that. He loved knowing that within an hour, thousands, if not hundreds of thousands of people would be looking at his dick.

It is what got him off.

It never failed to make him stiff, and today was no different. Stiff didn't quite touch it, to be fair. He was *hard*. The thought of that cute goth girl he'd just started following on the LifPic platform seeing his dick in all its floppy glory, sent surges of joy through his crotch.

Clive poked his head out of his bedroom and looked both ways down the landing.

The coast was clear.

At this time of night, no one would be up. His parents would be asleep by now, and his sister wouldn't be home. She never was these days.

He stepped out into the darkness, grabbing his crotch, a grin stretched across his face.

Tiptoeing towards the bathroom, he avoided the creaky floorboards and made it to his destination unobserved. Once inside, he locked the door behind him and undid his jeans, releasing his straining beast. He gripped it, and instantly, his legs buckled.

He closed his mouth and held his breath, straining to stifle the moan that was attempting to escape him. He didn't want his parents to come running to see what was ailing their child. The release was fantastic. It was dizzying, and in its own way, it was violent.

His love shot from the tip of his swollen head. It missed the toilet bowl completely, spattering the raised seat and cistern and even getting as far as the wall. Even though it only lasted a second, maybe two or three at best, it felt like a lifetime for Clive. He opened his eyes. Colours were spinning through his vision—shapes and patterns that would be unnatural in the real world. The purples and yellows merging in and out of each other made him stagger back a little and grin.

Clive loved everything about shooting his load. Even the adrenaline ebb that inevitably came afterwards. He could understand why they always depicted people smoking in bed after sex.

He hadn't tasted the pleasure of a real woman yet, but he'd watched enough porn to satisfy him until he could find someone with the same obsession and with as high a taste for it as he had.

Clive pulled away some toilet roll and wiped the tip of his wilting dick before slipping himself back into his jeans. He flushed, neglecting to wipe his spray from the seat and the wall. He didn't consider that his job, so he left the bathroom. This time, he strode boldly towards his bedroom, closing the door behind him, not caring if the way he slammed it woke his parents. This time, he had nothing to hide.

With his interest in the worst aspects of the internet temporarily waning, he reached over to turn off his monitor. He yawned, closing his eyes before snapping them back open when he noticed a small red number *1* next to his messages on LifPic.

He grinned when he saw who it was from.

Lil-Beth. The cute goth girl he'd been talking to and recently terrorised with a dick pic.

Another grin spread across his pasty face, and he clicked on it, ready for an outpouring of offence, disgust, and hate that would be focused on him. The thought of it all sent another tickling sensation towards his crotch.

The act of getting off on the disgust of others set the butterflies in his stomach flying.

His mouth fell into a pout when he saw the message was only a few words.

He had been expecting, or hoping, it would be a barrage of hate. One where he could almost feel the spittle from the person typing as they regurgitated their repugnance in his unsolicited entertainment. The butterflies stopped fluttering, and the rolling twinge in his crotch began to flitter away.

Neither sensation stayed away for long after he read the message.

>*Nice dick... wanna show me what else it can do?*

His grin widened slowly as he read, then re-read the words.

'*Nice dick...*'

He couldn't believe what he was reading. *Is she saying I've got a nice dick, or is she being sarcastic and saying it like* Nice, dick?

The tips of his fingers were tingling, and the butterflies were back, wreaking havoc inside his stomach. He had that weird feeling of not quite knowing if he needed to pee. Clive sat back at his desk and opened the messenger app fully. He looked at the words again. There was no comma between *nice* and *dick*.

Maybe she means it, he thought, not completely understanding what this meant.

>*Wanna show me what else it can do?*
What does she mean by that?

His brain wasn't functioning correctly. The messages were not connecting to his fingers, well, not in their full capacity. Before he knew it, he'd typed a reply and sent it.

>*It can do a few other things. Wanna see?*

Clive cringed a little. Although he thrived on the hate and venom he received from unhappy girls seeing his junk, he hated the idea of being taken for a ride. He sat, looking at the screen, willing for the grey tick to turn blue, signifying the message had been read. It was half a minute before he realised he hadn't blinked, and his eyes were getting tired. He rubbed at them, then realised his hands were shaking, too.

His throat was dry, but he didn't want to risk missing her reply while getting himself a glass of water.

'Come on... come on...' he mumbled, wiggling his mouse as much as he was wiggling his crotch. 'Come on, bitch!'

The blue tick came.

He thought his heart might explode, as it was beating that fast. It was thrashing so hard it was stealing his breath.

The chime came before the message on his screen appeared.

YOU HAVE ONE NEW MESSAGE.

He flexed his fingers, allowing the blood to run through them, as they had gone cold in the last minute or so. He licked the front of his teeth, closed his eyes, and took a breath.

>*Fuck yeah... I wanna see. Does it go any... bigger?*

As he read the message, his stomach flipped.

This is someone fucking with me, he thought. *It has to be, doesn't it?*

But a part of him still wanted to do it—wanted to shake his dong and let the blood flow do its thing. He put a hand down his trousers and grabbed his penis, squeezing the base. His other hand was on his keyboard, replying.

>*Your not fukig wit me r u.*

It was one-handed typing at its best.

He pressed SEND and quickly undid his trousers.

Clive played with himself for a moment until he grew a semi. He grabbed his phone, selected his camera, gripped himself at the base again, and snapped a few shots.

He thumbed through them, his sweaty fingers slipping a couple of times in the process. He picked one that made him look a little bigger than he actually was, selected it, added it to the LifPic messenger app, and sent it.

>*How does this grab you?*

He sent it before he could lose his momentum and courage.

He closed his eyes and screwed his face to match. Clive couldn't believe he was doing this. It went against all the codes of practice of the Legion of Dick Pic Senders—If there was such an organisation. He couldn't help but chuckle at the thought, making him feel a little better about what he was doing. He knew he wasn't alone in sending random dick pics to random women at random times... but he never thought he would find himself in a scenario like this.

Taking in a deep breath, he dropped onto his bed. He was trying to calm his frantic, heaving chest, but every nerve in his body was alive, tingling. Was she really into his dick? And maybe him, too?

He hoped so.

He closed his eyes, but not before giving his phone a quick scan to see if the blue ticks were back next to the message.

They were not there yet.

It was after midnight, and he had school the next day, so he attempted to sleep. Clive relaxed his body and forced himself to think pleasant thoughts. He'd seen Lil-Beth's profile picture online and liked what he'd seen. She *was* a cute goth, with enough pics of her out and about, doing stuff with other people, to know she probably wasn't some overweight forty-five-year-old man getting off on young boy's dick pics.

Clive imagined them together. She, taking pictures of herself, maybe inserting things into herself, like he'd seen on some of the more... extreme... websites he frequented. He imagined rude, filthy, disgusting, and degrading sex with her, her friends, and his friends.

This made him chuckle—he had no friends.

His phone chirped.

His dream of fucking Lil-Beth in a classroom, with the teachers tied up and forced to watch, petered out. His heart was thudding again. Clive hoped he might be able to slip back into that dream, as it was nice, in a romantic kind of way.

His instantly moist hand reached for his device, and he looked at it.

YOU HAVE A NEW MESSAGE, it read.

He clicked on it.

It was from Lil-Beth.

Instantly, his tongue stuck to the roof of his dry mouth, and he was immediately up off the bed. He opened the app on his computer and clicked the message. His breathing was rapid and shallow as he read the words. For a moment, or maybe two, they were just a jumble, nothing more than a scrawl across his screen. Eventually, they sorted themselves out and became legible.

He couldn't believe what he was seeing.

>*OMG, that's so fucking hot. You're getting me so wet. What else have you got?*

He was instantly hard again.

He couldn't believe this. He'd made a woman wet. Clive, the slightly chubby, fifteen-year-old virgin, had gotten the cute goth girl wet. He instantly thought of her squirting, like he'd seen in videos on the internet, as she rubbed herself off to his pictures.

He knew if he touched himself now, there was a real possibility of him going off instantaneously. He didn't want to do that. Not yet. Clive flexed his fingers rapidly over his keyboard and licked his dry lips.

>*Hell yeah, it does more... how about you send me something to think about, and I'll show you what it can do...*

He sent the message, scratching his nose and wiping the sweat from his face.

'Fuck, fuck, fuck, fuck, fuck...' he mumbled as the small grey tick turned blue instantly.

Clive held his breath, not wanting to move, just in case he creamed his trousers. Three dots appeared next to his message. She was replying. He clenched his fists until his knuckles turned white.

His computer and phone chirped simultaneously, showing the same screen: YOU HAVE A NEW MESSAGE! He clicked it, seeing a picture was attached.

It was a picture of a pair of breasts.

The image was grainy and dark as if it had hastily been taken in a girl's bedroom. They were small and perky, but to him, they were perfect. The two buds in the centre were small, tight, and dark. His cock tightened.

There was a message.

> *Your turn... I want to see you hard, rock hard!*

His hands covered his eyes, and his whole body tensed as he tried to stop himself from shooting off in his trousers. He held his breath until the feeling, the beautiful tingle, receded. Quickly, before he lost all rational thought, he freed his angry penis. This was the hardest he'd ever been, and it felt wonderful. Clive gripped his shaft, marvelling at the ivory beneath his hand, and with his other hand, he picked up his phone and took some snaps. He even took a little video of his hand moving up and down rapidly.

A little too rapidly.

A feeling like no other overcame him.

It started in his feet before spreading up his legs, then finally gushed out an eruption of cum from his swollen, pink head. The shot was so powerful it caught his chin. It seemed like nothing could stop it; it just kept coming. More and more and more. He realised he'd been edging himself for most of the night, and this was the result. His t-shirt was covered, and there was more dripping from his face. He wondered where else it had gone that he couldn't find. Grinning, he dismissed trying to find it. He just needed to send this video over to Lil-Beth. He knew she'd enjoy this one if she liked the others.

She was his kind of girl, after all.

Clive quickly uploaded it to the messenger application, wiping cum from his phone screen as he did. He pressed send. The anguish he'd felt earlier passed with each message he sent. He was confident she'd like this, and maybe... just maybe, she might send something good back to him.

He closed his eyes and prayed she would. Clive had no clue who he was praying to. He had a good idea that God, or Jesus, didn't grant prayers asking for fucked up photos or videos from girls, but it was worth the chance. *Nothing ventured, nothing gained,* he laughed.

>*I hope you like what you see... there's more where that came from if you can return the favour!*

The reply was almost instant.

Ping: YOU HAVE A NEW MESSAGE.

>*Fuck, you are hot... you are making me wide. Wanna see?*

'Do I want to see?' he asked out loud, looking over his shoulder to his bedroom door. The last thing he needed was his father bursting in, demanding to know what he was up to and what all the noise was.

>*What do you think?*

YOU HAVE A NEW MESSAGE.

He clicked on it. His breathlessness was back.

>*I want you to send me another pic, then I'll send you something I know you'll like.*

>*What do you want?*

>*Another vid. I want you to grip your cock so tight it turns the head blue. If you do that, I'll send you something HOT!*

Clive didn't have to think twice about it. This was the most fantastic thing that had ever happened to him, and he could already feel himself stiffening again. He opened his jeans and pulled them off. His crotch was still slimy from not cleaning himself properly after his last adventure, but it didn't bother him. This wasn't his first rodeo.

His dick was already semi-hard. He had never had a problem getting stiff again. His libido was strong. He was fifteen, after all. Clive knew when he found a woman to go with, he'd be able to satisfy her as many times as she wanted, *and maybe even some more even after that,* he added with a smirk.

Without giving it any more thought, he pulled his foreskin back, gave the white smegma that had built up beneath it a quick wipe, and grabbed the base of his cock. He then squeezed.

He gasped as the blood in his appendage swelled through every capillary in his organ. As it swelled, it sent a shiver through his whole body.

He pulled his foreskin as far back as it would go, marvelling at the small purple spots appearing next to his little eye. Breathing deeply through his nose, he squeezed again. The small dots began to grow.

Clive grabbed his phone and got it ready to take a photograph. He gave his cock one last squeeze and clicked the camera.

The relief as he removed his fingers from his shaft caused him to gasp. He bent over in his seat, panting as he looked at his erection. He hoped the little spots would have started to retract once the pressure had gone.

But they hadn't.

They were still there, staring at him, looking like something on the back of a cartoon dinosaur. He didn't care. Clive just wanted to get the shot up onto the messenger app and get whatever Lil-Beth was going to send back to him.

As he clicked SEND again, he felt as if he were on another level, a different plane of existence, like he was someone else, someone bigger, stronger, more Clive than Clive had ever been. He was laughing as the computer gave a WHOOSH to tell him the pic had been sent.

While he waited for the grey tick to turn blue, he looked down at his dick. It was bright red where he'd gripped it, and the head of the still erect member was a dirty shade of purple. His foreskin was still pulled back, and the frenulum, probably the only thing he remembered from all the time he'd studied biology—that, and the anatomy of a vagina—was pulled tight.

As he looked at it, he thought it was maybe a little too tight.

He was about to pull the hood back over his swollen glans when his phone and computer chirped in unison.

Suddenly his dick was forgotten about, and in his haste to open the message, he overreached the mouse on the desk. In his hurry to correct himself, he banged his erection on the edge of the desk.

A sharp, agonising pain tore through him.

Wincing and sucking in air, he looked down.

There was blood.

It was everywhere!

Panic!

Blind, agonising panic overwhelmed him. It overtook every desire he felt, and he almost bent double.

'Oh my God!'

The voice registered barely. Clive could hear someone speaking, someone in the distance, perhaps a million miles away from the emergency he was experiencing right here, right now. Blood was pouring. It was dripping down his still-hard shaft, pooling on his jeans, soaking into them. He knew they were ruined, but that was secondary to his ruined cock.

He was about to howl as waves of torment slathered him.

But something made him stop.

'That is so fucking HOT!'

It was a girl's voice, and she was speaking in an American accent.

His favourite of accents.

It dragged him out of the despair of his broken, bloody penis and caused him to glance at the computer screen.

He couldn't believe what he was seeing.

It was a pair of breasts.

A live pair of breasts.

They weren't naked, or on show, or anything like that, but they were doing their best to stretch a black and green striped t-shirt. Even through his anguish, he could see she wasn't wearing a bra beneath it. She was holding her phone or computer camera, and it was too low to see her face, either by accident or design. She was caressing one of her tits, tweaking the nipple.

The sharp agony was suddenly nothing but a dull ache.

'What?' he croaked, wondering if he'd heard her correctly.

'I said that's so fucking hot!'

He must have accidentally pressed the video call button in his overreach for the mouse. And she'd accepted.

'There's so much blood,' she whispered in a breathy, southern accent. Even though he was from Dudley, just outside Birmingham in the UK, he'd seen enough films to recognise a Southern American accent when he heard one.

'Show me!'

He didn't know if it was a request or a demand, but either way, it was odd. What was even odder was that he moved the webcam, with a blood-stained hand, down to focus on his weeping dick. Clive looked at the picture on his large screen, and the cut looked bad. The skin was hanging loose, and the blood poured from what he first assumed was his eye. As he saw it on the bigger screen, he realised it was coming from the foreskin.

This relieved him, but only a little, as the sting was on its way back.

'Get in closer to that blood. I want to see it dripping from your beautiful cock,' Lil-Beth whispered.

Clive couldn't believe what he was hearing. Even worse, he couldn't believe what he was doing. He pulled the camera closer to his dick.

'Grab hold of it. Grab hold of that fucking thing, will you?'

He swallowed and took hold of it as it was beginning to wilt. He winced as the agony took hold; it was probably the worst pain he could ever remember.

'Squeeze it again,' Lil-Beth whispered from his computer. He looked up, ready to tell her to fuck off, ready to disconnect the video, wake his parents, and get himself to the hospital. However, as he looked at the screen, what he saw made him reconsider everything.

She had removed her top, and her hands were touching and pinching her tight, dark nipples.

'What are you doing?' he asked. 'I... I think I need help.'

'Relax, Clive,' she purred. 'You're getting me so wet. I love all that blood.'

'What?' he croaked. 'What the fuck are you?'

'I'm horny, and *you've* done that to me,' she breathed. 'I want you to show me more. You like what I'm showing you, don't you?' As she asked, she gave a breathy gasp and pinched her nipples.

The twinge in his cock hurt, it made his eyes sting, but there was something different about it. It wasn't a bad hurt. In fact, the rush of pain felt kind of... nice!

A line from an old movie he'd watched once, or kind of watched just because it was on TV and had quite a bit of nudity, came to him. It was about a bouncer going to a new bar to rid it of all its low-life patrons. *Pain don't hurt,* he thought, with a smile, despite the torture.

'Oh yeah, Clive... grab it again. I want to see more blood. You show me the blood, and I'll show you more... of me.' Her voice was silky, it was lulling, and it was captivating.

He had no choice but to do what she instructed.

Clive wanted, or he needed, to see more of her. He didn't mind a little of the sweet pain he was experiencing. He just wanted more of her.

'Stroke it, Clive,' she whispered.

He did. Each time his stroke got to the bottom, and he pulled, more blood poured from the ripped skin, making his hand warm and sticky.

'Ohhh, I can fucking feel that, all over my tits,' she sighed. 'It's warm and thick. I think I can taste it.'

This was enough to get him hard again for the third time that night.

Although this wasn't a record for him.

'What... what does it taste like?' he asked, not understanding why, as he had never had any inclination to taste blood.

'It tastes like you...' she replied.

It wasn't what he was expecting to hear. The screen turned into a blur as Lil-Beth changed positions. He thought he caught a flash of long, dark hair that would match her online photographs. He also thought he caught a flash of lacy panties. This was more than enough for his libido to burst through the pain barrier and force his cock to go fully rigid again.

With the stiffness came more blood.

She groaned as she groped her breasts. One hand began to travel down the gentle curve of her stomach.

Clive had an idea where her hand was going.

'I need more blood,' she whispered, sounding as if she was right there in this bedroom with him.

'You want more blood?' he breathed.

'Fuck yeah. Give me more blood, you fucking animal.'

Clive liked being called an animal. He'd been called lots of names, usually from the victims of his random dick pic sessions, but this was different. This was on another level. This turned him on even more, perhaps a little too much.

He just wanted to give her more blood.

'How do you like this?' he whispered, surprising himself with the odd pitch of his voice. He pulled on his cock harder. The sting made his eyes water, but he wanted to draw more blood for her. The more blood he offered, the more she would reveal. He longed to see where her other hand was, what it was doing.

'I do like that,' she replied.

He yanked himself harder, again and again. With each stroke, he could feel the blessed agony of his skin ripping a little bit more.

'You know what would be on another fucking level?' she asked, her voice thick and sweet, filled with a sexy innocence he couldn't resist.

'What? Tell me, and I'll fucking do it. I want to see you though. I need more of you.'

As if obeying his demand, her camera tracked down her body, moving slowly down her stomach. He watched intently and caught a flash of the dark hair between her legs. As his eyes devoured the image of her beautiful thatch, he could feel himself almost ready to blow.

'Don't come yet,' she suggested. 'There's so much I want us to experience together.'

'What do you want me to do?' he asked, his breath almost stealing his words.

'Cut that fucking foreskin off!'

This should have been the end of it.

This request should have made him cut the connection. It should have waved the red flags, all the red flags that there were in the world, signalling that this was going in a wrong, unhealthy direction, and he should get the *fuck* away from everything unravelling here.

But it didn't.

And he didn't.

In fact, it did quite the opposite.

He was being carried along on a scarlet wave of what she was doing on his computer screen—and on the admission that he was really enjoying the pain.

Clive looked at his dick, at the bloody head poking through his tight fist. The skin flopping around, causing all the blood, was useless to him. He didn't need it. He knew loads of people who had been circumcised—well, he didn't actually *know* these people, but he saw them on porn videos all the time.

Maybe, if he rid himself of the skin, it would make his dick look a little bit bigger.

Maybe, when he sent more dick pics, it would get him noticed and appreciated a little more.

His face focused, his eyebrows ruffled, and his mouth screwed into a tight hole on the bottom of his face. Clive opened the top drawer of his desk. He knew what was inside, and he knew it was exactly what he needed.

Scissors.

His finger slipped from the holes in the handle as they were coated in blood, and it took him a moment to grip them. Eventually, he did, and he opened and closed them a few times, watching the blades slide past each other efficiently.

'What have you got there?' Lil-Beth asked. Her camera was back on her breasts.

He showed her the scissors.

'Oh!' she breathed, her voice sounding like Marylin Munroe in one of her ditzy blond movies that he'd wanked over a good few times. 'Are you going to do what I think you're going to do?' she asked.

Clive didn't answer. He just stood up, pointing his still bleeding erection towards the computer camera. It was out of focus, so he stepped back a little.

That did the trick.

She stopped wriggling and lay on her side. Her small breasts lolled to one side. She was fantastic, gorgeous, alluring. He knew she was watching everything he was doing.

Clive gritted his teeth. He took some of the flapping skin that used to be connected to the tip of his swollen gland and inserted one of the blades of the scissors underneath it. He took in another sharp breath as the cold metal touched his bloody cock, sending a shudder of erotic sensations through his legs.

'Do it...' Lil-Beth whispered.

He was hesitating.

'Do it... Let me see more of that sexy blood, you fucking beast!'

He bit down, clenching his jaw. He closed his eyes and brought the blades of the scissors together.

They were sharp, hardly ever used, and cut through the thin skin like he was cutting through raw bacon.

Colours flashed behind his closed eyelids.

The pain was fresh. It felt white, like it was pure—cleansing. It washed away the old pain and brought about a new regime of sanctified suffering.

He enjoyed it in a fashion.

Clive felt his legs buckling beneath him, and he staggered. As he did, the scissors slipped from his fingers. Holding his breath, he bent to pick them up, guessing where they might have fallen. He couldn't grip them again. Either they were too slippery, or his fingers were too wet with his blood.

He opened his eyes and looked.

It was both.

The sight of what he'd done to himself shocked him. It brought reality crashing back down upon him. *What the fuck have I done?*

His ruined dick was a mess of blood and limp skin, but somehow, he was still hard. *That can't happen,* he thought, having to bite his tongue to keep from passing out.

'Clive, you're the fucking best,' she said, her voice breathless. 'Watch this.'

Clive tore his eyes from his ruined appendage and looked at the computer screen.

The camera was panning down her body again. This time, it didn't stop at the thatch of dark hair between her legs. Her milky white thighs parted, and he saw it all. It was everything he'd wanted to see since this whole fucked up exchange had begun.

It was beautiful.

The delicate folds of flesh were pink and slightly swollen. As she shifted her legs, she pulled the camera closer, and her glistening lips pulled apart. The view was close enough to see the gossamer strands of her arousal juices bridging the gap between them.

His blood was forgotten.

Pain was a thing of the past. It was over the hills and far away, as they said in fairy tales.

'Do you like this?' she asked.

Clive nodded. He didn't know if she could see him or not, but he didn't care. His dick was rock hard again, ripping the already torn skin even further down his shaft, peeling it away like a wrapper from a melted chocolate bar.

He didn't want to touch himself for two reasons. The first was the agony of touching the raw, red flesh of his wound, and the second was because he didn't want to come yet.

His mouth was dry as he watched her fingers tickle herself. They came away wet, and once again, the strands of her arousal made silver strings from the beautiful, intimate flesh to the tips of her fingers.

The camera followed her fingers back up her body, leaving a trail of wetness in their wake. Clive longed to bathe in that wetness. He yearned to smell her sex; he'd have given anything at that moment to taste her.

Her fingers ran along her lips. She hadn't shown her entire face yet, but by the structure of her lips and the thick, red lipstick she wore, he knew it was her from the pictures she'd posted. Her mouth opened, the flesh battling to stick together as her lips parted.

His dick was throbbing.

Clive shivered as her tongue poked out from between her lips, and she licked her cum from her fingers.

He wanted to come then.

Clive needed to release everything building up inside him, to splash it all over her, even if it was just on the screen. He needed to anoint her with his love, his sex, his essence.

'Look,' she breathed.

Clive did as he was bidden.

Her hand pulled the devil horns gesture as if she were at a rock concert. The camera followed the hand as it traversed her body again, lingering on her tight, erect nipples. It continued further down where she lifted the two middle fingers.

'Do you want me to?' she whispered as the fingers tickled her clit. 'Tell me how much you want me to.'

'Fucking do it,' he croaked, his voice akin to the sound of tearing paper. 'Just fucking do it.' His heart felt like it was struggling to function, as his whole body was racked with shivers.

'You need to do something for me first.'

'A... anything,' he stuttered. 'Anything for you,' he finished in a whisper.

Clive couldn't believe what she was asking of him. He couldn't believe it was all so simple. Just one small thing, and he would be watching her delicate, dainty fingers delving between the wet, pumped folds of herself. He could witness them disappear into her warm, welcoming depths. He would watch as she slowly manipulated her swollen bud with her fingers, watch as she produced the thick white juices, letting them drip as she slowly brought herself to climax. All he had to do was one stupid thing.

It was all so fucking easy.

Without taking his eyes off the screen, he picked up the scissors as she had commanded. Breathing through his nose, Clive wrapped his hand around his cock. He no longer cared about the pain. He was beyond pain.

She had promised him pleasure to transcend all pain.

He was ready to do what was needed.

'Do it, Clive. Do it for me,' she purred, her voice rising and falling with each tickle of her clit. 'Say my name as you do it. Tell me you love me.'

'I... I love you,' he whispered. 'Lil-Beth, I do this for you. I love you; I always have.'

Clive plunged the scissors into the tip of his cock. It was a good aim as the blades sunk into the small slit on the tip.

As the sharp metal slipped into him, he came.

In that moment, the pressure he had been edging was released. Thick pink cum spat from his cock, shooting from between the metal blades. It wasn't the only thick liquid to explode from his member.

Dark, fresh blood came too.

It splashed his face. It entered his mouth, and he tasted an odd cocktail of blood and cum.

It wasn't as bad as he might have expected.

'Finish it,' Lil-Beth shouted. Her voice was orgasmic—like the prank video calls you got that turned the volume up high on your phone while a woman screamed in ecstasy, designed to embarrass you in public places.

The volume was up on his computer. He didn't remember putting it that high, but she was screaming the house down.

He knew it would wake his parents, but he no longer cared.

'Fucking finish it...' she demanded.

Clive closed his eyes and gripped the handle of the scissors protruding from the tip of his penis. He gritted his teeth. They were pink with blood-cum dripping from his mouth.

Her climax was reaching its zenith.

'Do it,' she whispered in the innocent way she'd spoken to him earlier.

With four deep breaths, he slipped his bloody fingers into the handles and pulled them apart.

The blades did their work.

They ripped through, destroying the shaft of his cock, tearing it apart.

Clive screamed as he sliced his dick, his one prized possession, his pride and joy, into long, fleshy shreds.

'Oh, Clive. You were so fucking good,' Lil-Beth whispered into her camera.

With a chuckle, she slipped back into her panties and pulled her t-shirt back on. She disconnected the camera from her computer.

She stretched her fingers until all her knuckles cracked, took a drink of water, and logged back onto the LifPic application.

The instant she opened the app, her computer chirped. YOU HAVE A NEW MESSAGE.

With a smile, she clicked on the message and took a long look at the attached picture. With a sigh, she clicked on the REPLY button!

Midnight at the Dead Dick, Fuck-hole Emporium

by Chuck Nasty

Earl Becker sat on the edge of the bed in the scuzzy motel room, taking the last few drags from his cigarette while chugging down the last drops from the silver can. To his left was a woman in her mid-twenties. Her body lay twisted, cattycorner on the bed, with her panties shoved in her mouth. A rope had been tightened around her neck.

While Earl had been sitting in a booth enjoying a whiskey and Coke, the brunette had stumbled into his arm, knocking his drink from his hand, bringing it to smash on the red-painted floor. The young woman turned to look. She was embarrassed at what her drunk ass had done, apologizing profusely. Earl saw no reason to be angry. He smiled, then offered the long-legged goddess with the hypnotizing chest a drink. She accepted. She accepted a lot—to the point of being trashed in Earl's motel room.

Earl had no real idea of what happened. Memories flashed through his mind, but not all together. The fact he'd killed her didn't bother him; it was that he couldn't remember doing it. This was his fourth kill. Usually, he wasn't drunk when he murdered. He wasn't even sure he'd wanted to kill this woman—it just happened.

Since this act of violence was random, Earl wasn't sure what his next step should be. There was the idea of digging into the trunk of his car for his usual tools and sawing her body up, stuffing the remains in baggies, and leaving them strewn throughout the county. The second idea was to leave her where she lay and get the fuck out of there before anyone suspected anything. He glanced at the clock. It was close to eleven PM. Surely, he could get out of dodge before anyone found the body. A grin spread across the bottom half of his face as a new idea occurred to him.

Earl walked out to his car to grab a bottle of bleach. He also wanted to take a quick view of the situation outside. There didn't appear to be anyone looming around. It was quiet as well. The only thing concerning him was the weather; the snow hadn't stopped for the past hour. It didn't show signs of slowing anytime soon, either.

After grabbing the bleach from his car, Earl hurried back into the room. With the snow coming down like it was, he didn't have much time to do what he wanted to do if he wanted to escape. He considered the upside of being snowed in with a dead body and all the necrophiliac fun he could have. Regardless, he preferred the idea of leaving.

Before making his grand getaway out into the winter weather, Earl grabbed the dead woman's ankles and pulled her body from the bed. She made a loud *THUD* as her purple-fleshed head smacked the floor, the rope still clinging to her neck.

Around the corner from the bed was the bathroom. Earl pulled the body across the floor. Her head dragged so hard against the filth-stained carpet that the panties he'd stuffed into her mouth to keep her from screaming were starting to fall from her dead pie-hole.

Earl grabbed her by her hair and threw her corpse violently into the tub. She landed with one leg draped over the tub's edge while the other stuck straight out. Her arms rested across her face. Looking down between her thighs, he saw a snapshot in his head of his face deep inside of her saturated cunt. He would have given her love-socket another pounding or two if he had more time.

Instead of wetting his dick with the juices of the dead, Earl decided to do the next best thing. He'd find whatever he could to shove up inside this woman's perfectly shaved little pussy and asshole. It was a diabolical idea, indeed. No matter to him, it just sounded like fun. He wanted to leave some type of sign that a psychopath had been there. By the end of it, there would be no mistaking that a psychopath had been there.

Earl flipped the young woman's corpse and bent her body over. It was hard to keep her dead weight steady, but he figured it would be a more accessible position to fit as much as he could into her pleasure canals. It was no easy task. The pose left her head smooshed against the bathtub knobs, with the faucet shoved in her mouth. Earl smirked when he heard her jaw shatter.

When the struggle of positioning the body in the tub was figured out, Earl grabbed whatever he could think of. He placed two fingers into his mouth to get them wet, then shoved them into her rectum. He slid them in and out repeatedly.

He grabbed the plunger next to the toilet and rammed it as far as it would go, starting in her anal cavity and popping out of her throat. This also helped keep the cadaver in a doggy-style position, even with the top half of her body wanting to fall forward more. The sounds of her innards being penetrated, bursting within her stomach lining, made Earl's cock hard. He had to fight the urge to rub one out.

Earl slid one of his hands under the corpse, rubbing and probing her vagina. He couldn't tell if it was natural secretions or blood, but he could feel that she was wet—not too warm, but that didn't matter. A shampoo bottle sat on the edge of the tub. Earl reached over, quickly grabbing it, then spread her dead vagina wide enough to fit the cap of the bottle in. He gave one mighty push and managed to make the bottle disappear. This made him snicker.

The conditioner was next. Earl used four fingers on each hand to spread the hole wider, causing a gash. Blood trickled from the torn flesh. He stretched her once-pretty pussy as far as it would go. It split several areas as more blood trickled out.

It became easier to load the dead woman's cunt with a toothpaste container, a bar of soap from the sink, a pair of nail clippers, and finally ending with the scrub brush used to clean the toilet bowl. He crammed that brush in there, violently scrubbing the inner walls of her packed vagina, pushing everything he'd already buried deep inside her deeper.

Blood and feces oozed slowly from her backside, around the shaft of the plunger. Earl gagged. The smell was horrendous. He realized his job was done as viscous fluids poured from her many holes. It was time to get the fuck out of there.

Earl took the bleach, doused the body, and splashed it around the room. He didn't worry much about his actions coming back to bite him in the ass. As far as the motel went, he never checked in with the same name.

His exit from the motel had been smooth. But getting far away from the motel—not so smooth. The snow had picked up even more, and he found it hard to see if he was driving in the correct lane. It had only been ten minutes since he'd gotten back on the road when his tires began to slip and slide. He realized he wasn't going to be able to travel much further.

There was a glimmer of hope. A sign in big, red letters read: DEAD DICK'S ADULT VIDEO STORE AND MORE. Being the kind of guy Earl was, he figured it would be a suitable place to lay low. During this type of snowstorm, there weren't going to be cops giving much of a shit about pulling people over—especially at a porn store.

Earl followed the sign. His beat-up Sentra slid into every lane as he tried to make it safely into the video store parking lot. There weren't many cars in the parking lot, but there were a few—secluded enough to hide, enough cars to blend in.

It was midnight.

Rushing to ease into an icy spot, he hadn't noticed the building. Earl turned the engine off and raised his head. *Holy shit! This place is huge!* In front of him was what appeared to be a large strip mall turned late-night porn vendor. Every window had been blacked out and boarded up.

Walking up the dark walkway leading to the entrance door, Earl was taken back by the almost haunted house-looking sign draped across the wall next to it. The large tarp showed a figure resembling Satan, with sunglasses over his eyes and surrounded by cartoonish characters of devil women. Earl grinned.

The large glass door read ENTER. Earl tried. The door wouldn't budge. He scratched his head, then tried again. *What the hell is wrong with this fuckin' thing?*

BZZZ!

A sudden buzzing sound came from a speaker above the door. "Welcome to Dead Dicks! Are you ready to get off?" asked a sensual female voice. Earl smirked again.

"Sure." He replied, staring up at the speaker.

"That's good to know. There are many ways to make that happen within these walls. Try the door again, handsome."

The door handle made an unlatching sound, and it opened slightly. Earl grabbed the handle and pulled.

Upon walking through the door, he found himself in a small foyer. The windows had been blacked out. He looked around curiously, wondering what he was about to get into. Earl had always been the adventurous type, hence the whole killing people thing.

BZZZ!

A glass door slowly opened in front of him. As it opened, a bright light came from the other side. A woman walked up to him. She was wearing a leather skirt with a top to match. Tattoos covered both of her arms, which were crossed, projecting her massive mammaries. Her black hair was held back in a ponytail. A smile crossed her face while her brows went down to a point.

"Welcome to Dead Dick's!" said a man dressed in a tacky Hawaiian shirt who came out of nowhere.

Earl jumped back. "Damn, man. What a way to give a man a heart attack!" he exclaimed. The man just stood there, gnashing a fat cigar between his teeth. "Who are you exactly?"

The man stood there, gnashing a fat cigar between his teeth. "Well, isn't it obvious? I'm Dick!" He laughed.

"Yeah, I guess that would make sense," Earl remarked, walking further into the establishment. The mood outside the store was completely different from the vibe inside the place.

"Now, seeing as you are a first-time customer, we need to go over the menu system here." Dick was a very excited fellow.

"Menu system?" Earl asked, raising a brow.

"Well, of course! How the hell will we figure out what's going to fit your fancy otherwise?" Dick gave Earl the impression he may have been a car salesman at some point in his life. Earl would be shocked if he hadn't. "So, here's the deal!" he enthusiastically shouted, handing a laminated paper to Earl. "On that menu, you will find many exciting offers to ensure you have a wonderful time here! See what looks good to you, and if you mix and match, I'll give you a deal you can't refuse!"

Earl took his attention off the six-foot bald man to examine the paper in his hands. *It must be the worst menu I have ever seen.* He couldn't help but chuckle as he read the lists of what was offered. Some stuff wasn't that unusual, while every few lines, a curve ball would be thrown, and something off the wall would be listed. *Full Tug, full suck, missionary, doggystyle, glory-holes.* Earl took his free hand and combed his fingers through his sweaty hair. "So, this isn't a porn store?"

Dick's demeanor changed. "Oh, yeah. We do that too." He reached down and flipped the menu that was in Earl's hand. There were titles upon titles of adult features to rent, buy, or watch there. Next to where it said WATCH IN STORE, it also read PUT ON A FLICK, SOMEONE'S SUCKING DICK. The phrase was off-putting. Earl knew what went on in those kinds of places. There were usually little rooms in the back where truck drivers and horny old men would cozy up to each other, watch porn and end up swallowing each other's meat sticks. Not a fiber of his being wanted any part of that shit.

"Go back to the front. I can tell you aren't thrilled by our 'movie list' and all its perks." Dick Laughed, and a weird twinkle shone in his eye as Earl flipped the menu back over and surveyed the list of fantasies and kinks.

"What's the 'What the Hell? Special?'" Earl looked up from the menu to Dick, who was shaking his head, still gnashing the cigar, smiling from ear to ear.

"A bit of an adventurer, are you?" Dick asked, removing the cigar from his mouth, exhaling a cloud of smoke.

"I guess you could say that."

"Perfect! Many of our customers love this offer!" Dick placed an arm around Earl's shoulder. "You see... what's your name again?"

"Earl."

"Excellent! Earl!" He laughed. "Well, you see, Earl, this is exactly as it states. It's a 'what the hell?' scenario. We have taken the whole right side of the building and turned it into a mash-up of kinks. This is only for the strong. No weaklings allowed, if ya know what I mean. And I think you do." He smiled at the leather-clad woman; she smiled back.

"So what? I go back there and put my dick inside a bunch of glory holes without any idea of what's on the other side?" Earl wished his interest hadn't been piqued, but it had. There wasn't much to worry about. If this place were running some weird prostitution ring, they wouldn't want any attention brought to it. *The worst thing that might happen: a truck driver plays with my dick for a minute.* The thought made Earl want to puke. "When you say a mash-up of kinks, does that mean everything?"

"Well, there are glory holes, if you will, back there and..." he paused, smirked, then resumed, "Everything? Probably not. However, there's a fucking lot!"

"Jesus. There are women back there, right?"

Dick and the leather woman both cackled. "No worries. There are women back there, I assure you. But tuck in those insecurities. You gotta be open-minded!"

Still feeling the booze from earlier, his judgment was probably off more than it should have been when making such a decision. Part of him thought the whole thing was sketchy as fuck. But the desire to release the sexual mojo he'd built up, shoving all those items into the dead girl at the motel, outweighed his apprehension.

"Fuck it. How much?"

Dick seemed pleased. He walked over to the register sitting atop a glass case full of dildos and porno flicks. Taking his finger, he searched through a pricing list taped to the countertop. "Since you are a first-timer, I will take off a chunk, making the total only two hundred dollars, my friend."

"Why am I doing this?" Earl said out loud as he dug through his wallet, pulling out two one-hundred-dollar bills, and handing them over to dick, who popped open the register, shoved in the money, and pulled out a key.

"Here you are!" he said, handing the key to Earl.

Earl shook his head in disbelief at his strange reality. "Thanks. So where is the start of this sex gauntlet," he joked.

"Candy, take our friend here down to the start of the fun." Dick smiled while speaking they wouldn't want any attention brought to it. *The worst thing that might happen: a truck driver plays with my dick for a minute*. The thought made Earl want to puke. "When you say a mash-up of kinks, does that mean everything?"

"Well, there are glory holes, if you will, back there and..." he paused, smirked, then resumed, "Everything? Probably not. However, there's a fucking lot!"

"Jesus. There are women back there, right?"

Dick and the leather woman both cackled. "No worries. There are women back there, I assure you. But tuck in those insecurities. You gotta be open-minded!"

Still feeling the booze from earlier, his judgment was probably off more than it should have been when making such a decision. Part of him thought the whole thing was sketchy as fuck. But the desire to release the sexual mojo he'd built up, shoving all those items into the dead girl at the motel, outweighed his apprehension.

"Fuck it. How much?"

Dick seemed pleased. He walked over to the register sitting atop a glass case full of dildos and porno flicks. Taking his finger, he searched through a pricing list taped to the countertop. "Since you are a first-timer, I will take off a chunk, making the total only two hundred dollars, my friend."

"Why am I doing this?" Earl said out loud as he dug through his wallet, pulling out two one-hundred-dollar bills, and handing them over to dick, who popped open the register, shoved in the money, and pulled out a key.

"Here you are!" he said, handing the key to Earl.

Earl shook his head in disbelief at his strange reality. "Thanks. So where is the start of this sex gauntlet," he joked.

"Candy, take our friend here down to the start of the fun." Dick smiled while speaking to the woman in leather.

"Come on, handsome," Candy said, taking Earl by the hand and leading him around the corner into the main lobby of the building.

Earl was amazed as he peaked through the doorway leading to the main showroom. It was huge. On one side of the room, the wall was covered in adult DVDs, and the other side was full of classic VHS titles from porn history. Earl noticed an old VHS copy of *Behind the Green Door*. *Holy shit! I haven't seen that one in years. Probably one of the creepiest fuck flicks from the seventies.*

In the middle of the lobby was an upscale-looking bar. Behind the counter, lights above and below illuminated the many bottles of expensive alcohol. A flat-screen television was mounted above the back wall amid the bottles. Earl guessed the screen must have been at least sixty inches. He looked at Candy, who giggled at his amazement. "Hey, how big is that TV?" he asked.

"I have no idea. If I had to guess, I'd say sixty," Candy answered as they approached the bar.

Knew it!

A chandelier hung from the ceiling above them. In front of them was a big black door. As they walked toward the door, Earl glanced at the whiskey bottles on the left side of the bar. "Is there any way I could get a drink or two before I go in?"

"Of course! We want you to feel good. Why do you think we have this here? A little liquid courage should enhance your journey." Candy walked behind the bar and grabbed a shiny glass. "What's your poison?"

Earl watched as Candy leaned down to get a scoop of ice. Her cleavage was a pleasant sight. Her leather top looked as if it were going to fall. He had his fingers crossed. "Whiskey on the rocks, please."

"Coming right up." Candy grabbed a bottle behind the bar and poured the brown liquid into the glass. Earl took the drink, gave the dangerously sexy woman a nod, and put it to his lips. In less than a minute, there was only ice remaining.

Earl belched. "That hit the spot!" he exclaimed, placing the glass on a metal coaster. He was startled when Dick's overly excited voice blared into his ear.

"Are you ready, Earl?" Dick said, then rubbed Earl's shoulders like he was a boxing coach or something.

"Hey, now!" Earl shrugged Dick's hands off. Dick jumped back, glaring into Earl's eyes.

"No need to get hasty, buddy! We are all here to have a good goddamn time! So, let's do that. Candy!" Dick snapped his fingers.

The black-haired beauty walked out from behind the bar, again grabbing Earl by the hand.

"Hey, I'm sorry, man. I get jumpy," Earl said as Candy led him to the big, black door.

Dick waved a hand, giving his best fake smile.

"So, how does this work exactly?" Earl asked as Candy placed a key into the hole above the doorknob.

"When you walk through this door. You are going to have a seat in front of the flat screen. Once a fetish is completed, a new door will unlock. Then, you move on... providing you can even keep going." Candy giggled. "That key you were given will get you into the last fetish room, as well as the exit." She turned the key, unlocked the door, and led him by the hand.

Earl got a foot inside the door when one last question occurred to him. He quickly looked back at Candy. "Hey, what happens if I can't finish a room?"

Candy blew him a kiss. "Don't pussy out, and you won't have to find out." Suddenly, her arms shot out, and she pushed Earl the rest of the way through the door.

The door locked behind Earl as he stared into the darkness. *Did I fuck up? I think I may have made a mistake.* Realizing he may be in over his head, he turned around and started to beat on the door. "Hey! I think I made a fuck up! Let me out!"

Dick's voice blared from a speaker. "Sorry, Earl. You see, I forgot to mention that all sales are final, and there are only two ways out, and backing out isn't one of them. Have fun!" There was a pause. "Now, go sit the fuck down!"

Earl turned his head and noticed a viewing seat in the corner and a flat-screen TV in front of it. He apprehensively crept over to the uncomfortable-looking pew. As he sat down, he looked at the screen. *The HD on this thing is unreal.* The screen was solid white. A tall woman wearing a long red dress with the sides cut up the thigh, showing off toned legs, came into view. The woman's hair appeared naturally red, with lipstick to match. *She has a whole Jessica Rabbit thing going on. I can dig this.*

The camera view panned over to show a naked man sitting on his knees with a ball gag in his mouth. Blood poured from a gash in his brow. His hands were cuffed behind his back, and he appeared to be crying.

The redhead looked into the camera. "If you are sitting in that seat, it means you must be new here. No one ever comes back twice."

"Fuck," Earl muttered.

"See this piece of shit?" the camera zoomed in on the man, only showing him from the neck up. She started talking to him like he was a dog. "Oh, look at you. You little piece of shit. Bad boy, you are. We are going to show the newbie what happens to pieces of shit." The camera zoomed back out, showing the woman in full view. She had her breasts out, tweaking her nipples with one hand and rubbing between her legs with the other.

This is about to get interesting. Earl wasn't expecting what came next. The camera zoomed in, only showing her tits and above. Her fingers pinched down hard on her nipples. She had a look of pleasure on her face—the type of pleasure brought on by pain.

Earl noticed that one of her hands was no longer playing with her fake tits. He could see she was doing something off-camera with her other hand. As the camera zoomed back out, Earl's eyes became huge as the shot revealed the woman was stroking a very stiff, massive, and engorged penis between her legs. The camera panned out more as she strutted toward the man.

The man tried to beg with the ball gag in his mouth, but it only came out as spitty mumbles. The red-headed woman walked out of view for a second, then returned and displayed the shiny, sharp-looking knife she held to the camera. The blade clearly wasn't made for hunting. It had a black handle covered in spikes, made to inflict pain.

The cameraman's hands got shaky, making it momentarily hard for Earl to see what was happening. When the picture became clear again, the camera was zoomed out enough to show that the redhead had ripped the ball gag from the man's mouth and was violently assaulting his throat. She plunged the depths of his esophagus with her massive member. The man's eyes leaked water as they rolled into the back of his head. His handcuffed hands tensed as he tried to rip from his shackles. "You piece of shit!" She pulled her cock from his mouth, and saliva slapped to the floor below them.

Earl watched closely as the helpless man looked like he wanted to fall over. Every time the poor bastard got smacked in his face by that bitch's colossal cock, Earl couldn't help but laugh.

The redhead quickly turned her attention to the camera and winked. Then, while stroking aggressively with one hand, she raised the knife with the other and brought it down, slicing into the top of the man's head. His body convulsed as blood splashed out. She removed the blade and ran it across his throat. Crimson sprayed her engorged member, and she let out a moan of pleasure as ropes of semen splashed the man's dying face. There was so much blood that Earl couldn't look away.

"Hey, Earl?" She spoke Earl's name.

"Shit."

Out of nowhere, a hidden compartment opened in the wall beneath the flat screen. The woman in red leaped out.

Earl screamed as she grabbed him by the arms. From her face down, she was covered in red. "How funny is it, Earl? This could be you!" She laughed.

"Get the hell off me!" He shouted in her laughing face before pushing her onto the floor. Earl realized that the head of the man from the TV was still impaled around the woman's gargantuan meat pipe. "Jesus fuck!"

"Have fun, baby!" the redhead crawled back into the opening, then slammed it closed.

Earl heard the mechanical click as the next door—the gateway to whatever madness lay ahead—unlocked. *I don't want to keep going.* Earl stood and stared at the door, which was cracked and waiting for him to open it all the way. "Hey! Dick! Let me out of here! Keep the fucking money. I don't want to be ripped apart by a six-foot transwoman! Okay?"

"Earl, you know I can't let you out." A soft-spoken Dick came over the speaker again. "Here's a little motivation for you." Another secret latch opened. An angry, muscular rottweiler stared Earl down. "If I were you, I'd get to moving, fuckface."

"Nice puppy." Earl shivered as the dog snarled at him. "Oh, come on!" The dog galloped towards him. The only place to run was through the next door. He bolted for the door and threw himself through, practically diving into the next room before slamming the door behind him.

"Oh boy," he muttered, looking around the new room he found himself in the middle of. There were no screens. This made Earl even more nervous. The walls were painted pink. Two more doors were on each side of the farthest wall. The lights weren't blinding but bright, like stage lights, shining down at the mystery doors.

Big fluffy couches lined the room. Earl thought the best idea was to hide behind one of them before whatever was behind those doors came out. Gripping the material of the giant couch, he thought it felt like a large marshmallow as he ducked down by its side.

When the doors unlocked, Earl couldn't see what was walking out. He sure as fuck heard the footsteps, though. Slowly, he lifted his head to peak from the side of the marshmallow couch. *Just when I think things couldn't get weirder...*

Standing on the other side of the couch, Earl saw two individuals dressed in animal costumes. One was a yellow rabbit, while the other was a blue bear. Both sported combat boots and bandanas around their fuzzy heads. *Great! Furry Rambos...*

The sight was disturbing enough to make Earl even more nervous. The rabbit held a steel mallet, large enough to need both hands. The bear was gripping a machete. *Well, this is truly a nightmare.*

Earl had been in many sticky situations, but this was a whole new ball game for him. He watched where the furies were stalking. He scaled the back of the couch, trying to remain hidden long enough to figure out his next move.

SLAM!

The yellow rabbit came over the top of the couch, slamming the mallet down on Earl's shoulder. Bone shattered as it made contact also. He fell face-first onto the floor.

"Jesus fucking Christ!" The injured side of his body pulsated with pain.

The furies laughed from under their masks.

The blue bear appeared above Earl and kicked him in the face before he could move out of reach, crashing him back to the floor. Blood shot from his nose as he went down. He glanced up in time to see a machete swing down at him. Rolling to the left, he narrowly avoided being chopped in half. The blade sparked as it hit the concrete floor with a loud CLANG.

The kick to the face caused Earl's vision to blur. He could tell the room's color had changed from pink to red. His body was lifted, and the bear tossed him into the corner.

"You fuck!" Earl cried out, spitting two teeth from his mouth. He could barely move but was able to turn in time to see both evil fucking furies lurking toward him. The top half of his body throbbed, and his face bled from multiple contusions. As bad as it hurt, Earl mustered his strength to lift himself off the floor.

"You ever been fucked by a furry before, Earl?" the rabbit asked, then launched the mallet in the terrified murderer's direction.

"Shit!" Earl shouted, almost taking a love tap from the giant mallet head. It smashed into the wall instead of his face. He was about to limp away when he saw a moment of opportunity. The bear was heading to the wall to retrieve his partner's weapon. Earl leaped at him, knocking them both onto the floor. With balled-up fists, he hammer-punched the disturbing character's chest. Earl relished the groans accompanying each blow as they issued from behind the fucker's mask.

The blue bear swatted at Earl but missed. Earl supposed the drawback of being a killer furry would be the difficulty the costume added to getting up and fighting back. Earl brought one last fist down, busting through the cheap mask. He grinned as he felt his knuckles smash the person's nose.

Glancing at the reflection in the broken eye of the bear mask, Earl saw the damn bunny raising the machete, about to bring it down onto his neck. When it came down, Earl moved, and the blade wedged into the bear's throat. The bunny struggled to remove the machete from the almost-severed neck.

Earl raced to the mallet stuck in the wall. The bunny was preoccupied with sawing the machete blade from the bear's throat. Blood sprayed with every sawing motion. A final red geyser spewed from the bear's neck as the blade came free, and his head rolled to the side.

With both hands, Earl gripped the handle of the large mallet and pulled it from the wall. The timing was perfect. As he freed the mallet from the wall, the bunny swung the machete. The hammer side of the mallet knocked into the machete and sent it flying across the room.

The evil bunny panicked, unable to take two steps before being met with a blow to the back from Earl's mallet. As the bunny flew forward, the mask flew off. "Shit. Shit. Shit," a female screamed.

Creeping up to the bunny, Earl got a laugh, watching as the woman in the bunny suit tried to get up from the cold floor. Laying on her back was as far as she got. Then, it was like watching a turtle flipped on its shell. She looked up at him, grinning from ear to ear.

"What are you smiling about?" he asked.

"It doesn't matter what you do to me. You are going to suffer regardless." She laughed hysterically.

Earl shared her grin as he brought the mallet down on her face. A piece of her face chipped away with each repeated blow. By the end of it, her head was a bloody pile of brain matter, skull fragments, and mashed flesh.

The sound of a door unlocking caught his attention.

Moving to the right, he located the door, which was hidden by how the room was painted. The only way to tell a door existed was when it would unlatch and creak open a little.

Earl couldn't deny he was more nervous than he'd ever been before he started his trek through the kink factory. Hell, the only thing he'd worried about before was being raped by a dude or something. But judging by what he'd already experienced in the brief time he had been there, he knew he was bound to get fucked in more ways than he could imagine.

Dragging the mallet behind him, he slowly approached the door.

The loudspeaker was flipped on again. "Ummm, sorry, bud. No weapons can be taken to the next room."

Earl shook his head, trying to disobey.

"Wouldn't do that if I were you," Dick said.

"Fuck you!" Earl shouted, putting his free hand on the doorknob.

TZZZ!

A shock came from the knob, stunning his entire body. The mallet dropped from his hand. He let go of the doorknob.

"Now. Enter. Play nice, asshole." Even though Dick maintained a chipper tone, there was irritation hidden between words.

Not thrilled at having to move on without any protection, Earl grabbed the doorknob again. This time, nothing shocking happened. The door pulled back smoothly as he moved to the next room.

This room was smaller than the last. Where the previous room was as big as a two-car garage, this room was the size of a master bedroom with high ceilings. Like the main lobby, a chandelier hung from above. It may have resembled a nice bedroom, but there was no bed. In the middle of the room were three stirrups. The sight piqued his interest, knowing it couldn't be anything so delightful.

A door in the corner of the purple-painted room opened. If it were someone's bedroom, it would be where a walk-in closet or a bathroom would usually be. Earl's eyes grew large as he watched three beautiful women walk out, each wearing only bikini bottoms.

The first woman to walk out looked to be in her early twenties, with short blonde hair, porcelain skin, and the cutest little A cups Earl had ever seen. It was drafty in the room, colder than the others had been, and each woman's rock-hard nipples pointing in front of them confirmed the temperature.

The woman who walked out after the blonde was a little thicker in size. Dark, wavy hair hung down past her shoulders. Earl wasn't sure of the size of her breasts, but he knew they were bigger than double D's. She gave him a wink as she headed to the stirrups.

The final woman to walk through the door didn't appear as full of life as the other two. They both were smiling and shaking their tits around, but not this one. Her hair was in braids, and the color was a mess. It was like she had dyed her hair too many colors at once. The tattoos on her arms, showing images of moon signs, pot leaves, and Grateful Dead bears, led Earl to believe she was some kind of hippie. Like the other two, she was also a gorgeous woman. However, she looked ill. Her skin was sickly pale—almost gray.

Each woman stood next to a stirrup.

The loudspeaker clicked on again. "I can see you are a little more at ease with this one so far, Earl. Well, I just wanted to come on and let you know that you shouldn't put your guard down just yet." Dick laughed. "Ladies, please take your positions."

Each woman slid off their bottoms, tossing them to the side. Earl grinned like a kid finding a Playboy for the first time. He couldn't help but be visually stimulated. The thicker woman had a thin layer of hair on her pubis (the landing strip), and the blonde was smoothly shaved. The hippy, however, showcased an unruly, unkempt bush.

When the three women climbed up, placed their legs into the stirrups, and spread them, Earl shuddered in his skin. Nothing appeared too concerning when the Thicker, dark-headed beauty spread her legs. He glanced over at the blonde, noticing a string dangling from her fuck socket. *That's promising,* he thought to himself, shaking his head. There was something physically wrong with the hippy chick, though. She was shaking. Her eyes rolled back in her head.

"Hey Earl! You like eating pussy?" Dick hollered over the loudspeaker.

Out of nowhere, Earl was grabbed by two individuals and then received a swift kick to the back of the leg. He fell to his knees. As he was picked back up, he saw the two people detaining him were muscle-bound men. They were dressed in leather with leather masks to match. Both had zippers over their mouths.

The men dragged Earl to the stirrups where the thicker girl was spread out. One man shoved Earl's head down into the woman's crotch. He gave it a quick look and still couldn't find anything wrong with her pretty pussy.

"Eat it!" the masked man holding his head down commanded.

When Earl was about to oblige, Dick's voice echoed from the speakers once again. "Meredith, why don't you spread that pretty peach open more."

The woman did as she was directed. She smirked at Earl as she used her fingers to spread her sex wider. A flood of white fluid gargled out of her. "Ever wonder what a twenty-man creampie looks like close up?"

Earl swung his arms around violently, trying to pop one of the masked men in the face—no such luck. The men were bigger, not to mention much stronger than he was. The man holding him by the neck squeezed tighter, sinking his fingers deep. Earl already knew what was coming next.

The big-handed man shoved Earl's mouth into the river of semen flowing from Meredith's vagina. He gagged as he felt the warm goo touch his lips.

"Eat it!" the other masked man demanded, grabbing him by the face and prying open his mouth. "Lap it up, big man!"

After being physically forced to slurp up most of what was pouring from between those thick thighs, the men let go of Earl, allowing him to fall to his knees and puke up a belly full of man-snot. He wiped his face with his sleeves. Then it was back to work.

The blonde leaned back, a warm smile running from ear to ear. Her eyebrows came down to a point. She ran her fingers down her naked breasts, leading them down to the clean-shaven pink paradise between her legs. Earl smiled at her, face still dripping slime, forgetting the atrocity he'd just been through. Then he remembered the string he'd noticed dangling from inside her shaven haven.

Following her hands with his eyes, he remembered why he was concerned about this one. Her nimble fingers swiftly plucked the string and yanked out a blood-soaked tampon. One of the masked men gripped a chunk of Earl's hair, pulling him closer. The blonde grabbed him by the jaw, pried his mouth open, and shoved the saturated tampon down his throat.

Earl gagged, watching in horror as she reached down again, pulling out another soaked tampon. It looked more decrepit than the previous one—like it had been marinading a while.

Earl gagged again, coughing up the first tampon from his throat. However, before he was able to spit it out, the blonde shoved the browner-looking tampon into his mouth, pushing the first one back down his throat. He could feel the vomit rising from his stomach. This routine went on for another two minutes. One after another, the blonde pulled out tampons like a clown with colored handkerchiefs, shoving every last one of them into Earl's mouth.

Both men standing behind him shared a laugh when they threw Earl to the ground to puke once again. Holding himself up by his hands and knees, an overload of used tampons fell from his mouth. A few didn't want to come out, and if the vomit didn't push them out, he retrieved them with his fingers, causing more vomit to spew from his lips.

In short order, the men lifted him again. This time, he found himself in front of the sickly-looking hippy with the killer bush. There was something wrong with her. She lay there moaning with displeasure.

"For fuck's sake! Don't make me do it!" Earl screamed, seeing that hidden beyond the valley of hair was a very infected-looking vagina.

Earl fought hard, making it difficult for the men to keep a hold of him. One grabbed one arm while the other did the same on the other side. They twisted his arms, forcing him into a bent-over position. In his history with women, he had been with some questionable and downright disgusting women. But nothing compared to what his eyes beheld. This giant gash of a love socket was green with infection, dripping odorous pus, and writhing with maggot-looking worms. Tiny insects milled about on the layer of scabs crusting her thighs.

Earl's gag reflex returned with a vengeance.

"Last one, shithead! You're almost free!"

"Goddammit," Earl muttered, shying away from the gross gash.

The hands on his face and neck were too strong. As they forced him to place his open mouth over the wet, worm playground, the hippy began convulsing—then suddenly stopped—*as if things couldn't get worse!* The feeling of his lips resting around the open hole while bugs wandered around on his tongue was the most horrifying and disgusting thing he'd ever experienced. Then something started to fill up his mouth.

"Swallow it!" the masked man on the right demanded.

The taste was like snot pouring down his throat, and the smell was pungent. Earl jerked his body, trying to get free, and failed. However, as the men struggled to keep him tame, they lost some of their grip. He was able to remove his mouth from the infection zone, turn around, and spit the neon green substance into one of the masked men's eyes.

Earl was quickly met with a punch to the face, knocking him away from the men. He looked at the hippy girl. She was dead. Worms fell from her spread legs onto the floor, which was already covered in a cocktail of human fluids.

The masked men charged at him.

"Stop! You know what? Let him go on to the next round. This one leads to the end, you sick fuck!" Dick's cackles could be heard throughout the entire building.

The masked men stopped, turned to their left side, and marched out of the room. There was no unlocking sound, but the next door was noticeable when a spotlight turned on above it. Remembering the key he'd been given, he pulled it from his pocket and staggered to the door.

By this point, Earl was disoriented. The intoxication he'd entered with had become a hangover. He'd been beaten and had his mouth raped. It was time to get the fuck out of there.

The key fit as he slid it into the hole. The lock turned. Excitedly, he swung the door open, hoping to see an EXIT sign shining in his face. His expectations were too high.

In front of Earl were two ways to go. On one side was a green wall with multiple holes in it. The other way led to a giant black metal door. A strong odor lingered from the door's direction. He looked in the room with the holes. There didn't seem to be any way out from there.

Making a split-second decision, he ran to the black door. It looked more like the door of a bank vault. There was no doorknob, just a big metal wheel that needed to be turned.

Earl hoped to open the door and find an easy kink waiting for him as a reward for all his hard work getting to the end. Such was not the case. It took all his energy, but he got that big bastard of a door open. The smell burned his nostrils. The sight before him was something he never expected.

It was a pool. There was no telling how deep it was. It was full—but not full of water. It was shit! Human feces, no doubt. But that wasn't all... Chunks of human flesh and limbs floated in the bog. Earl noticed the head of the guy who got face fucked at the beginning of the whole nightmare.

Being so grossed out, he missed the guy dressed in leather standing in the corner, lathering himself up in fecal matter. "Come on in. It's so warm and squishy. You want out, don't you?"

The words made goosebumps spread across Earl's skin. The way out was somewhere in that room.

Earl had his nose pinched, but the fumes still managed to invade his sinuses. "Fuck this! I am not swimming in shit, Dick!" Using both hands, he slammed the black metal door.

Dick didn't say a word, just laughed over the speaker.

Earl stomped to the wall filled with holes. *Maybe one of these holes would open a way out. What if this is just a choice of what's a worse way to be free?* In the middle of the wall was a note. All it said was PICK A HOLE. It could only mean one thing.

Without hesitation, he pulled his cock from his pants and plopped it into the closest hole. The feeling of wanting to collapse rushed over him. His head felt dizzy. As he stood with his flaccid penis dangling within the green wall, something started playing with it. Fingernails combed the shaft back and forth. It felt nice—relaxing even... until it was sucked into someone's mouth and bitten.

A wail of torment escaped Earl's mouth as he pulled back, seeing his pathetic meat stick was no longer where it was supposed to be. All he had now was a bloody stump, which bled like a stuck pig, soaking the wall in crimson.

He started crying and fell to his knees, inadvertently placing his face in front of one of the holes. As soon as he did, the end of a double-barrel shotgun poked through, emptying both barrels into his face. The explosion of Earl's head sent a splatter in every direction. Brains, blood, and flesh painted the ceiling and floor.

"Okay, people. We got another sick fuck moron coming in. Dump this pile of shit where shit goes. I'm sure the septic man would love a new plaything!"

Blood Harvest
C.A. Baynam

As the sun dipped below the horizon, casting long shadows across the forest floor, Amelia's car rumbled along the winding road into the heart of the secluded town. The dense canopy overhead seemed to swallow the remaining traces of daylight, enveloping her in darkness.

The town appeared like a forgotten relic from a bygone era. Dilapidated buildings lined the narrow streets, their windows shattered and doors hanging off their hinges like gaping mouths frozen in silent screams. The air was thick with an unsettling stillness, broken only by a crow's distant cawing and leaves rustling in the breeze.

Amelia parked her car near the town square. Her footsteps echoed ominously against the pavement as she stepped into the chilly night air. A sense of unease settled over her like a suffocating blanket.

Drawing her coat tighter around her trembling frame, Amelia approached the nearest building—a rundown tavern with faded paint and boarded-up windows. As she pushed open the creaking door, the hinges protested loudly.

The tavern's tables and chairs were scattered across the dusty floor. The air was thick with mildew and decay, mingled with the faint tang of something metallic. The smell made Amelia's stomach churn with dread.

Amelia made her way to the bar, where a lone figure stood silhouetted against the flickering light of a dying candle. The bartender, a grizzled man with sunken eyes and a face weathered by years of hardship, regarded her with curiosity and suspicion.

"What brings you to our little town, *stranger?*" he asked, his voice barely above a whisper.

Amelia hesitated for a moment, "I'm a journalist. I'm here to investigate the disappearances plaguing your town." She extended her arm as an offering to shake the man's hand.

The bartender's expression darkened. His face filled with disgust as his eyes squinted with suspicion. "You'd do well to mind your own business, *missy,*" he growled, his voice laced with warning.

Amelia swallowed hard, feeling the weight of the bartender's gaze bearing down on her. She squared her shoulders, refusing to let the fear clenching her heart show on her face. "I'm just trying to understand what's been happening in this town," she said, her voice steady despite the uncertainty running through her veins. "People have been disappearing, and no one seems to know why."

The bartender's lips twisted into a sneer. His eyes glittered with a dangerous light. "Disappearances, you say?" he muttered with disdain. "And what makes you think it's any of your concern?"

Amelia met his gaze head-on, refusing to back down. "Because people have a right to know the truth," she replied firmly. "Whatever's going on in this town, it's not right. I can't just turn a blind eye to what's happening here," she continued, her voice rising with determination. "Someone has to speak up for those who can't speak for themselves."

There was silence for a moment as the bartender regarded her with contempt. Then, with a dismissive wave of his hand, he turned away, muttering something under his breath that Amelia couldn't quite catch.

Amelia drove to the outskirts of the town, where she stumbled upon an old, abandoned warehouse hidden amidst the overgrown foliage. The building loomed before her, its windows shattered, and its walls marred with graffiti that seemed to writhe and twist in the moonlight.

Fear gnawed at her guts as Amelia pushed open the rusted door and stepped inside. The air was thick with the stench of mould and something far more sinister. The cloying odour made her skin crawl.

As her eyes adjusted, she saw a makeshift altar adorned with blood-stained symbols and the charred remains of long-extinguished candles. Surrounding the altar were rows of crude wooden benches, each coated in a thick layer of dust and grime.

Amelia approached the altar, her pulse accelerating with fear and excitement. Her footsteps echoed loudly against the cold concrete floor. With trembling hands, she reached out to touch the blood-stained symbols. Her fingers traced the intricate patterns with a sense of morbid fascination.

As she examined the altar more closely, a sinking feeling settled in her stomach—she was not alone. With sudden dread, Amelia whirled around to find herself surrounded by shadowy figures. Their eyes gleamed with malice in the moon's light.

As the figures shambled closer, Amelia's scream echoed throughout the building. Her cry went unnoticed as their hands closed around her. Their touch felt icy against her skin.

With a surge of adrenaline, Amelia fought back with all her might, her fists flailing as she lashed out at her assailants. Their grip only tightened. Their fingers dug into her flesh with vice-like strength, threatening to crush her bones.

With a guttural growl, one of the figures leaned in. Their breath was hot against her ear as they whispered words of an ancient language she didn't understand. It was no use. She was overwhelmed by the sheer number of them. As they dragged her towards the altar, Amelia's heart pounded in her chest with a frenzied terror. The sight of the blood-stained symbols and the charred remnants of candles filled her with dread.

"Looks like we've got ourselves a little troublemaker," one of them sneered as he dragged her down. The others chuckled darkly. Their eyes twinkled with perverse delight at her suffering.

The cold stone floor pressed against her knees as they held her before the altar. Tears streamed down her face as she pleaded for mercy. She watched as the others came closer, sinister grins on their faces.

Amelia struggled to break free from their grasp. She screamed and kicked at them as they pushed her down. One man pinned her head down with his foot, mashing her face into the concrete. As they bound her with ropes, her cries were drowned out by their jeering laughter. A cloth was forced into her mouth and secured with rope.

Amelia's world spun in a haze of terror and pain as she was dragged out of the warehouse and into the deserted streets. The cloth muffled her cries as the rope held it tightly in place, digging into her gums behind her teeth. The ropes scraped her flesh, leaving angry welts as they bound her hands tightly behind her back.

The townsfolk surrounded her as they dragged her through the desolate streets. Darkness closed in around her. The town hall loomed ahead like a beacon of despair, its doors hanging off their hinges.

Amelia trembled with fear and exhaustion. Pain shot through her legs as she was pushed to her knees. The council of elders loomed before her like dark spectres, their hooded figures casting long shadows that seemed to dance and writhe in the flickering torchlight.

Their eyes bore into her with disdain and amusement. Amelia could feel their gaze like a physical weight pressing down upon her, crushing her spirit with its evil burden.

"You dare to meddle in affairs that do not concern you, outsider," one of the elders shouted, his voice dripping with contempt. "You have trespassed upon sacred ground. For that, you must pay the price." He motioned to one of the other men to remove the cloth from her mouth.

Tugging her head backwards, he roughly pulled it from her mouth.

Amelia swallowed hard, her throat dry and constricted with fear. "I... I was only trying to uncover the truth," she stammered, her voice barely above a whisper. "People have been disappearing, and no one seems to know why. I had to do something."

The elders exchanged a glance, their hooded faces unreadable in the dim torchlight. "And in your arrogance, you thought yourself worthy of uncovering the secrets of our town?" another elder sneered, his voice like a dagger twisting in Amelia's chest.

"We have lived in harmony with the darkness for centuries," another elder added, their voice a chilling whisper. "But you, an outsider, have disturbed the delicate balance by just being here. What did you think you were going to accomplish? For that, my dear lady, there can be no forgiveness."

Amelia struggled, screaming as the townsfolk tightened their grip. Their fingers dug into her flesh like talons. Her screams pierced the air, but the townsfolk remained unmoved, their faces twisted as they tore at her clothes with savage fervour. "Please, no! Stop!" she begged, her voice raw with desperation.

"The balance must be restored. He demands a sacrifice, and she will be the vessel through which it is appeased."

"You cannot do this!" she cried. "I am not your *sacrifice!*"

"Silence her," one of them commanded. With cruel efficiency, the cloth was forced back into Amelia's mouth and secured tightly with rope.

As Amelia's screams turned into muffled sobs, one of the men walked towards her, a knife in his hand, and cut through her clothes. She frantically kicked at them, trying in vain to stop them. The blade slipped a few times and sliced through her skin. But her efforts were futile against their overwhelming strength.

They laughed as they ripped her pants from her body.

The men dragged her past the elders towards an altar at the back of the room—a grotesque monument of twisted wood and bone adorned with carved symbols. Naked and exposed, Amelia's body trembled at the sight of it.

"The sacrifice must be pure," one of them intoned.

Another elder nodded in agreement, his sinister eyes gleaming. "The blood must flow freely," he murmured. "Only then will he be satisfied."

The men forced Amelia's body against the altar. The rough edges of bone poked into her back. She frantically struggled against them as they bound her, but it was useless—they were too strong.

The townsfolk formed a circle. Their faces twisted into grotesque masks of anticipation as they chanted and incanted in their strange language. Amelia's heart raced as she listened. The hairs on the back of her neck stood on end as she felt the presence of something stirring in the darkness. She could feel its thirst for blood and pain reaching out for her.

Amelia's eyes widened in terror as an older woman broke the circle. Her movements were slow and deliberate as she approached with a gleaming knife in her hands. Amelia's heart pounded in her chest as the woman drew closer.

When she reached Amelia, the woman's wrinkled face twisted into a heartless smirk as she leaned in and kissed Amelia's forehead. The touch of her lips was cold and clammy against Amelia's skin.

Before Amelia could react, the woman plunged the knife into her side with a swift, brutal motion. Pain erupted through her body as she cried in agony.

As the woman withdrew the knife, Amelia's vision swam with tears. Her breath came in ragged gasps as she struggled to comprehend the horror of what was happening to her. But before she could fully grasp the situation, the woman leaned in once more, kissing her cheek with a sickening tenderness before sticking the knife into her again.

The second woman stepped forward. Her eyes leered with hunger. As she took the knife from the first woman's trembling hands, her fingers curled possessively around the hilt.

"My dear, sweet Amelia," she purred, her voice smooth and honeyed with a hint of malice beneath the surface. "I am honoured to make your acquaintance."

The woman placed her hands on Amelia's breast, gently stroking her skin. She moved her hand upwards to her face, slid her fingers into her mouth past the rope, and roughly plied it out of Amelia's mouth.

Amelia recoiled from the woman's touch, trembling with fear and disgust. "Who... who are you?" she whispered.

The woman smiled a twisted grin. "I am Lilith," she said, her voice echoing through the Town Hall with shrill authority. "And you, my dear, are about to become a part of something truly magnificent."

Dread threatened to consume Amelia whole as she watched Lilith raise the knife to her and hover it inches from her skin.

"And now, my dear," Lilith whispered against Amelia's ear, "let us begin." She thrust the knife into Amelia's trembling flesh, each stab sending shockwaves of pain rippling through her body as she cried out in agony. She slid the knife into Amelia's thigh, dragging the blade upwards, slicing through muscle and tendons as she held Amelia in a hugging embrace.

The elders stood at the head of the altar, their faces shrouded in shadow as they raised their hands in supplication. "Behold the sacrifice," one shouted, drowning out Amelia's begging. "May her blood appease the ancient ones and bring their wrath upon our enemies."

Amelia's eyelids grew heavy, weighed down by the agony pulsating through every fibre of her being. Each breath felt like a searing inferno, her lungs screaming for relief as she fought to keep herself from succumbing to the darkness. The pain was a relentless onslaught, ruthlessly tearing through her very soul. She could feel the heat of the flames licking at her skin, and she writhed in agony.

She fell into unconsciousness.

When she awoke, the room was dark. She was alone, with nothing but the echoes of her screams.

As Amelia's eyes opened, the first rays of morning light pierced through the cracks of the Town Hall's boarded windows. With a groan, she attempted to move, only to find herself bound tightly to the altar of wood and bone. She tugged against her restraints, but they held fast, cutting into her swollen wrists and ankles as a cruel reminder of her captivity.

The two women who had stabbed her walked through the door, followed by a few other townsfolk. They grinned menacingly when they saw her. Predatory excitement flashed in their eyes.

"We thought you might be awake," Lilith, the elder of the two women, purred as she slowly approached.

Amelia's heart pounded in her chest as she watched them draw near.

"What do you want from me?" she whispered, her throat raw from screaming.

Lilith's grin widened, "Oh, my dear, we have so much planned for you," she said, her voice a sickening blend of sweetness and cruelty. "But first, we must prepare you for the next stage of the ritual."

Amelia tried vainly to loosen the straps and break free. She was too weak. The townsfolk watched in silent fascination.

Lilith and the other woman closed in, brandishing their knives maliciously. Lilith leaned in and whispered, "You belong to us now, Amelia." Her voice dripped with venom. "And there is no escape from the darkness that awaits you."

The other woman nodded hungrily as she raised her knife. "Prepare yourself, dear," she cooed, her voice sickeningly sweet. "The real fun is about to begin."

"The last part of the ritual is clear, Amelia. You wanted to know what happens to outsiders who come here. You thought people had a right to know. *Do you think that now, Amelia?*" Lilith walked around the altar. "You should have left. Len told you not to meddle in things that do not concern you. But alas, you didn't heed his warning."

"Now you will stay," the other woman sang as she sat at the altar's base.

"Please... don't," Amelia pleaded.

"It's too late for pleas, dear," Lilith sneered. "You belong to us now, body and soul."

The other woman nodded eagerly, her knife poised to strike. "The darkness demands a sacrifice," she intoned, her voice a chilling whisper. "And you, dear Amelia, are now the chosen one."

Lilith poked Amelia in the ribs repeatedly with the knife, each jab deeper than the last. Amelia screamed as she felt the knife puncture her flesh. She felt blood trickling down her sides.

The other woman, now on her knees, brought her knife up from Amelia's ankles, slicing her open. Blood sprayed in gory arcs as both women slashed her flesh with savage brutality, carving deep wounds that gushed crimson with each merciless strike.

"Lorraine, look," Lilith called out to the other woman as she grabbed a handful of Ameila's hair and yanked her head back.

"Please...stop..." Amelia cried with tears streaming down her face.

Lilith and Lorraine laughed sadistically, their faces twisted in primal ecstasy. Lilith shoved her knife into Amelia's mouth, pushing it back as far as she could. The blade sliced through each side of Amelia's lips, tearing through her cheek muscles.

Amelia's vision blurred with tears of agony as the knife was mercilessly yanked from her flesh. She screamed in a sudden burst of defiance, her voice raw with pain and fury. Bloody spittle flew from her lips, landing on Lilith's face.

Lorraine moved in a swift, savage motion. Her blade slashed across the soles of Amelia's feet with a sickening crunch. Amelia's screams reached a crescendo of agony as fresh waves of pain consumed her, sending shockwaves through her torn body.

Blood dripped beneath her mutilated feet, pooling on the stone floor. Every nerve in her body screamed with unbearable torment. Every breath was a ragged gasp torn from the depths.

Lorraine stood and faced Amelia, their faces almost touching. Blood smeared on her face as she leaned in and kissed Amelia. Licking her lips, she savoured the metallic taste. She smiled at Amelia and cupped her breasts, squeezing. "You'll make a good mate. Beautiful firm breasts he can play with to keep busy." Bending down, she took Amelia's nipple in her mouth. She gently suckled for a moment, teasing the nipple with her tongue.

Amelia was revolted. As she struggled to remove her breast from Lorraine's mouth, pain surged through her body like lightning. She let out a piercing scream, looking down at Lorraine, who was kneeling in front of her.

Lorraine's laughter echoed through the hall as she savoured the taste of flesh between her teeth. Blood ran down her cheeks in thick rivulets, staining her quivering lips a crimson hue. With a sickening satisfaction, she stood up, her eyes alight with sick delight as she toyed with the mutilated remains of her victim.

She poked her finger into the gaping hole where Amelia's nipple should have been and pushed her finger in as far as it would go.

But before the madness could escalate any further, a voice cut through the chaos like a knife.

"Enough!"

The male elder's voice rang out. Behind him, the townsfolk followed silently, their faces covered in expressions of anticipation and dread. "I would apologise for the suffering you have endured," he intoned, his voice dripping with wicked satisfaction. "But the truth is, I enjoyed every moment of it."

She struggled against her restraints, her voice hoarse with desperation as she begged for mercy. "Please, let me go! I haven't done anything wrong!"

The male elder's voice echoed through the Town Hall. "Enough!" he bellowed, his tone sending trepidation into the souls of all who heard it. His gaze swept over the townsfolk, his eyes cold and calculating. "Lock the doors," he commanded.

As men moved to obey his orders, panic spread like wildfire among the townsfolk, their cries of terror and hopelessness growing louder with each passing moment. Some pounded on the locked doors, their fists bruising against the unforgiving wood.

The elder remained unmoved, watching with a look of numb indifference. "No one will be leaving this room," he declared. This is the will of the darkness."

"I know there are non-believers amongst you. Now, you will leave this flock. How you depart... *Only he can decide.*"

From behind the altar, in the shadows, grotesque figures emerged. Their bodies rippled and shifted with unnatural motion. Their skin stretched taut over sinewy muscles pulsing with otherworldly vitality. Eyes glowed with eerie luminescence, casting light that hauntingly illuminated their grotesque features.

Claws extended from gnarled fingertips, sharp as razors and dripping with the blood of countless victims. Their mouths stretched into menacing smiles, revealing rows of jagged teeth that gleamed with a sickly sheen in the moonlight.

As they descended upon the townsfolk with mad ferocity, the elders looked on with horror and fascination, their eyes wide with delight.

With each savage blow, the townspeople were torn apart. With brutal efficiency, limbs were torn from sockets, and entrails spilt to the ground in a grotesque display of violence. Blood sprayed in all directions, painting the ground a mosaic of burgundy and gore as the creatures ravenously feasted upon their victims. A chilling silence descended upon the town, broken only by the sound of flesh being torn and bones snapping.

Lorraine laughed, her voice a twisted melody of madness as she danced amidst the slaughter. Her hands were stained with blood. She embraced the darkness as she stared at Amelia, taunting her with the knife.

Amelia's stomach churned with disgust as she watched Lorraine and the gruesome scene behind her. Her mind struggled to process the carnage she was witnessing.

As the last echoes of the townsfolk's screams faded into the night, Amelia came to terms with a bitter realisation. She was trapped in a nightmare from which there was no escape; no one left would ever help her.

The elder's voice cut through the eerie silence following the slaughter. He stared piercingly at Amelia as he addressed her. "You see, my dear Amelia, we had no choice but to rid ourselves of the non-believers," he began, his voice low and measured. "They sought to deceive us, to pretend to be something they were not. And for that, they deserved to die in such a manner."

"How could you do such a thing?" she demanded, trembling.

The elder remained impassive as he continued to speak. "The ritual we performed tonight is a sacred tradition passed down through generations," he explained, his voice tinged with grim reverence. "It is a way for us to commune with the darkness, to appease its hunger and ensure our continued prosperity."

As he spoke, the elder's eyes gleamed with fanatical zeal, his belief in the ritual's importance unwavering. "But for the ritual to be successful, we require a sacrifice," he continued, his tone taking on a sinister edge. "A willing participant who will offer themselves up to the darkness, surrendering their soul in exchange for the favour."

Amelia's blood ran cold at the realisation of what the elder implied. "You want me to be the sacrifice," she whispered.

The elder nodded, his eyes burning with chilling intensity. "My dear Amelia, you talk as if you have a choice. You *are* the sacrifice," he replied, his voice soft but filled with stern certainty. "With everything Lilith and Lorraine have done to you, do you honestly think you're capable of escaping us now? You are the key to our success, Amelia. With your sacrifice, we will ensure the continued prosperity of our town."

The gravity of the elder's words bore down on Amelia like a leaden weight, crushing her with the realisation of her dire predicament. She struggled against her restraints, her heart pounding in her chest as she faced the chilling truth of her role in the elder's twisted ritual.

"I won't be a part of your sickening ritual," she declared, her voice trembling with defiance.

The elder's expression remained stoic, unmoved by her outburst. "Your fate was sealed the moment you set foot in our town."

The elder's eyes gleamed as he regarded her with frigid detachment. "You are an outsider, Amelia," he replied, his voice tinged with malice. "...a threat to our way of life—to the delicate balance of our world. And for that, you must be sacrificed."

The others had left the Town Hall, leaving Amelia with Lorraine.

As Lorraine loomed over Amelia with a predatory glint in her eyes, she reached out with slender fingers, tracing a jagged line along Amelia's cheekbone. Her touch was like ice against Amelia's skin, sending pangs of dread down her spine.

With a twisted smirk, Lorraine leaned in close and whispered. "You thought you could escape, didn't you?" she hissed, her voice dripping with venom. "But there's nowhere to run, nowhere to hide."

Amelia's breath caught in her throat as Lorraine brandished the knife.

With a sickening smirk, Lorraine circled the altar like a vulture, her movements graceful yet filled with sadistic intent.

"Maybe this will be a lesson for you not to meddle in things that don't concern you. Well, I suppose it's not really a lesson to you because you'll no longer be here," Lorraine taunted. With a deft flick of her wrist, she slashed at Amelia's hands and fingers, each cut sending searing waves of pain lancing through her body.

Amelia screamed in agony as her fingers were torn from her hands, the sound echoing off the walls of the Town Hall. Blood splashed up the back of her legs and dripped down the altar.

Lorraine stepped back, *"Now, undo those ropes!"* her sadistic laughter filled the hall.

Amelia's heart pounded in her chest, each beat a desperate plea for escape from the encroaching darkness. With every ragged gasp, she fought to keep her head upright. Her muscles screamed in protest.

Behind her, the darkness loomed like an evil spectre. Its presence was palpable in the air as its sinister whispers filled her mind with dread. She could feel its icy breath against the back of her neck.

From behind her, talons emerged from the shadows. Their razor-sharp points sunk cruelly into her flesh. Searing pain surged through her abdomen as she cried out. Amelia's screams pierced the night. Panic and terror overcame her as the claws dug deeper into her flesh. Physical and mental agony radiated through her body.

She fought against the talons' vice-like grip with every ounce of strength she could muster. The more she struggled, the deeper they sank into her body, swiftly tearing through muscle and sinew.

Amelia's flesh tore away with sickening squelches, exposing the raw, bloody mess of her insides. Bones cracked and splintered under the pressure, sending shards of agony shooting through her body with every movement. Her vision swam with pain and shock as she watched hands tare at her ravaged body, stripping away layers of skin and muscle until there was nothing left but a grotesque pile of gore at her feet.

With one final, gut-wrenching scream, Amelia's world faded. As the darkness closed around her, she knew her torment was finally ending.

Or was it...

Acknowledgements

I would like to take this time to thank each and everyone of the authors that took time out, to write a story for this sick and twisted anthology.

And, of course a big thanks, must go out to our Editor Sidney Shiv, for working his ass off to get this ready.

Oh, and let's not forget Christy Aldridge, who has to put up with me near enough every day, for her amazing covers.

So thank you Christy and Sidney.

A big thank you goes out to you, the reader. For picking this book up and taking the time, to come on this twisted journey with us.

Massive thanks to you all.

Made in the USA
Columbia, SC
01 June 2024